LATOYA GETE

Copyright© 2023 LaToya Geter
Published by Re'Nique Publishing
All Rights Reserved. No parts of this book shall be duplicated, distributed, reproduced, or photocopied without permission from the author.

This is a work of fiction. All characters, events, incidents, and places are from the author's imagination. The characters are not based upon actual persons, living or dead. The resemblance of actual persons living or dead is coincidental.

Dear Reader,

I would suggest you read books II and III before reading this book. There are mental health issues within this book. Suicide does occur.

Thank you so much for your continued support of the series.

Happy Reading,

-Author LaToya C. Geter

LATOYA GETER

Dedicated to women who love their partner despite the things they can't control.

THE RECIPE OF A GODLY WOMAN IX: HOPE

Audrey

My husband and I were so happy that our children were almost out of the house! Three down, and the twins to go! Malachi, our entrepreneur, was doing well with his technology service business. He was known around Crestview for fixing technical difficulties. He even contracted with a few companies. He was forever a mama's boy! Nothing was changing that! He would beat his father to bring me lunch or a gift on my birthday or Mother's Day.

Ariel was a college graduate and art teacher at her elementary school in Crestview. She never gave up drawing. She was a young entrepreneur as well. My baby sold her paintings throughout Crestview and was nationally known. Her work was throughout our house. We supported her. We supported each of our children. Ariel made it a point to stop by and see her daddy every day! I think she just visited me because I lived there. She was the ultimate daddy's girl. Their relationship grew more after Daniel decided to give her his last name. Her father gave up his parental rights to her years ago. He did not fight the consent. She became a Reynolds, and years later, Arbrielle and the twins were born.

Arbrielle was our singer! She was a gospel recording artist, and I was so happy to see one of my daughters following in my footsteps of singing for God! Even though she had my talent, she and I were like oil and water! As she became older, we did not mix. Daniel often said it was because we are so much alike! She, like Ariel, loved her father! They often fought for his attention as children.

DaNia was the oldest twin. She was everything I was and more. She also was the mommy's girl. The one who latched onto my leg, screaming like somebody was trying to snatch her on the first day of school. The one who did not like to share me with her sisters or brothers. The one who stayed wearing my clothes and shoes. The one who had to call every day or send me a text. DaNia was an aspiring actress. Ariel and Arbrielle had a positive influence on her. DaNia believed that if her sisters mastered their choice of arts, she could too. She was enrolled in the theatre program at Ross and Stone University. Of course, the school was not far from her mommy!

DJ was different. My son was not a mama's boy or daddy's little man. As a child, he loved reading with me and fishing with his father and brother. As a college student, he would bring me flowers and sail with his father. Like his twin sister, DJ was enrolled in Ross and Stone University. As the oddball, he was enrolled in the physics program. His father and I were not complaining about his aspiration to be a data scientist.

Here is DaNia's story...

THE RECIPE OF A GODLY WOMAN IX: HOPE

DaNia

The vibrating of my phone woke me up. I didn't open my eyes, but I was up. When my phone stopped vibrating, I knew it would start right back up again, and it did. My eyes opened, staring at the ceiling of my dorm room. There was no need to roll over to see who was calling me. Me and my roommate already knew who it was. We were used to my phone vibrating on the small two-drawer dresser after midnight. We could expect it to go into the early morning hours if I didn't answer. *Putting it on silent, I was too afraid to do that. Something could happen, and I would blame myself for not being there.*

My roommate knew the situation. She was kind enough to understand. I knew other people would complain. So, after my first year at Ross and Stone University, Symone agreed she would be my roommate until we graduated. We were juniors, and she still supported me through the early morning calls.

I was still staring at my ceiling by the third set of calls. I heard Symone say,

"Nia, if you want me to answer it, I will."

Still staring at the ceiling, I said,

"Don't. I'm gonna answer."

Rolling over in my twin-size bed, I saw Symone had rolled over, looking my way. The time on the purple table clock on top of my small dresser read two in the morning. My phone screen told me I had an incoming call from *Bestie Bae.*

My mama's best friend is my Auntie Lauren. Me and my siblings grew up around her kids. We called them our cousins. As we grew up, we realized we weren't biological cousins. My aunt's son, Gregory Jr, also known as Lil Greg, became my best friend. Along the way, we started to develop feelings for one another. Lil Greg was a year older than me. He was at East Crestview High before I was. When I got there, we started dating. Things were always good between us. His father was released from prison during his junior year of high school. Lil Greg already told me how he felt about his parents' relationship. He hated what his mother went through. He remembered seeing his father beat my auntie Lauren. He wished things could have been better between his parents because he loved his dad. He felt like his dad was taken away from him. Lil Greg had a relationship with his stepdad, my uncle Cornelius, but it was nothing like his relationship with his dad.

Not only did Lil Greg have conflicting feelings about the entire situation, but he also struggled with his identity. He always strived to do his best or beyond his best. He was afraid he was going to be like his father. My Auntie wasn't the breadwinner, but my uncle couldn't handle that. She had a consistent job as an entrepreneur with her salon. Uncle Greg was always from job to job. The outside world didn't know what was going on in their household, but Lil Greg and his older sister Layla knew.

THE RECIPE OF A GODLY WOMAN IX: HOPE

While trying so hard not to be his dad, while missing him, Lil Greg's mood changed. He was either depressed or extremely over the top. There was no in-between. The night terrors he would have didn't help his mental state, leading to him calling me. I always answered because he also struggled with suicidal thoughts. I hated seeing him going away to an institutional facility for months at a time. That was another reason why I picked up the phone when he called.

I picked up the vibrating phone from the small dresser. I pulled the covers back from my body as I answered my phone. I knew the routine. I got out of bed.

"Hey, babe."

I put the phone on speaker for Symone to hear as I walked to my closet space on my side of the dorm room. I listened to Lil Greg while pulling down a gray hoodie to throw over the pink cami I wore with black leggings.

"I need you, baby," he said to me.

"What happened?" I asked him, sliding into my purple crocs.

"A nightmare. I don't wanna be here. Like, what's the point? I'm just like my dad. You're in college. I ain't gonna be able to support you."

"Don't talk like that," I said to him.

The way his extremely unpredictable behavior was, his therapist recommended individuals from his support system be on Life 360 with him to monitor his locations. He chose Auntie Lauren and me to be on the app. I opened the app to see where he was. He wasn't too far from campus.

I picked up my keys from my dresser. Symone whispered to me,

"Be careful."

I walked over to her and hugged her. With Lil Greg still on the phone, I went to our dorm room door, opened it, and left.

I followed the Life 360 app, meeting Lil Greg at a local park. I pulled onto the parking lot in my Toyota Camry. I could see him standing in front of his black Dodge Charger. He was leaning on the hood. I parked my car next to his and got out. Looking over the roof of my car, I could see he had his head down with his hood on. I walked over to him, eased between his legs, lifted his chin, gently pushed back his hood, and eased my hands around his lower body. Leaning in and hugging him, I felt his arms wrapping around me. Resting my head on his chest, I asked,

"Do you wanna talk about the nightmare?"

"I didn't have a job he said," beginning to tell me about the night terror. "Nobody was hiring me. Then, I was standing in front of a mirror, looking at myself. I turned into my dad. I looked down. My mama was beaten and bloody in my arms."

Easing up from his body, I saw tears falling down his face. I wiped his tears and said,

"I hate you had that nightmare."

"I love my mama. I would never hurt her."

"Of course you love her. I know you wouldn't hurt her. When you're unconscious, your negative thoughts get the best of you at night. Did you take your night meds to help you sleep?"

Lil Greg shook his head no. *My will of care fell a little.* I was always there to help him. I didn't like to hear that he wasn't taking his medication. The meds would help ease the nightmares. There was no need to ask him why he didn't take his meds. I knew why. He hated to be on the medication. Even though they helped him, he didn't want to rely on them. I understood that he didn't want to become dependent on the medication. At the same time, I was honest and truthful with Lil Greg. The truth was he wasn't always compliant with therapy. He went, but he missed a lot of days. When he went, he would tell me he didn't want to talk about seeing his mother beaten or his true feelings about himself, especially being named after his dad.

"When you get home, you should take your medicine," I told him.

Lil Greg ignored me. He went right into,

"Seeing you helps me feel better."

I smiled at him.

"I'm glad I could help you."

He ran his finger down my cheek.

"I like seeing you smile."

My smile eased away as I looked down.

"You like to see me smile, but I don't like to see you sick like this. You used to smile. You used to be happy. Now you're down and sad most of the time."

"Blame my parents."

My eyes filled with tears. I gulped, holding them back. Yes, his parents' relationship was traumatic for him and his sister. He couldn't blame them forever. He could try harder if he wanted to. My tears were because I knew he could do well in therapy. *I tried my best to be hopeful.* I couldn't ignore my fears. I was afraid he was starting to decline. My major fear was that he wouldn't get better.

"Do you want to talk about your parents?" I asked him.

He quickly gave me a hard "No."

"Alright," I said, backing off the subject.

"I just need you," he said.

I looked into his now somewhat enlarged, bulging, glossy eyes. *They concerned me.*

"As long as I have you, I'll be fine," he said.

I ran my hand down his cheek, remembering when he was calmer and peaceful. That was before his dad came home. The selfish side of me wanted Uncle Greg back in prison. At least I would have my best friend and gentle soul back. My hopeful side took over, and I could hold on until he started to work on his issues.

THE RECIPE OF A GODLY WOMAN IX: HOPE

Professor Jett Davenport

My eight in the morning theatre improvisation class was small. Unlike my other classes, I didn't have to take roll. There were twelve students in the class. Walking in, I greeted my students like I did every morning. I noticed one student was missing. DaNia Reynolds.

DaNia always sat by Taylor Fletcher. Some days, they came to class together. On other days, they left together. Maybe she knew where DaNia was.

"Miss. Fletcher, have you heard from Miss. Reynolds?"

"I haven't," smiled Taylor.

"I don't want to start without her."

DaNia wasn't the student who missed class. When absent, which was rare, she would send an email. In less than twenty-four hours, I would have a documented excuse. I hadn't received an email that morning.

I could wait a few minutes. I paired my students with one another for five-minute improvs. My students had the opportunity to review the details of their assigned commercials. That was also my way of giving DaNia more time to show up.

We were coming up on seven minutes of waiting. I stood at the podium, looking out at my students, reviewing their commercials. I heard the door at the back of the classroom open. I rose my head to see DaNia coming into the auditorium. She looked different this day. She wore jeans with a nice blouse or a neutral dress on a typical day. She never wore bright or neon colors. Black and white wasn't her thing, either. Natural shades of browns, nudes, and pink seemed to suit her. *When she walked down the far right aisle of the auditorium in a pair of gray leggings with a red hoodie, I knew something was off.*

As I knew she would, she sat next to Miss. Fletcher.

"Good morning, Miss. Reynolds," I said, greeting her.

She lifted her head. *Our eyes connected. I gave her a light smile. She matched my smile with a small one.*

"Good morning, Professor Davenport."

"I'm glad you made it. We were waiting on you."

Her hand rested on her chest in surprise.

"You didn't have to wait on me. I'm sorry."

"No need to apologize. Just perform like we all know you can."

She smiled and gave me a nod. The entire theatre department knew how talented DaNia was. She wasn't just talented because she was a part of the Reynolds family that had been through Ross and Stone. She was the student who took feedback from staff and worked it into her acting style, which made her the most versatile actress we had ever seen at Ross and Stone.

The first five years I had been teaching at Ross and Stone, I didn't have a student who could top her match DaNia's gift. My colleagues had been there longer than me. They claimed DaNia was one of a kind. No student in the department's history could be compared to her.

DaNia

Every day, I had a morning class. Some students hated eight o'clock classes. I didn't mind. I liked to get my classes out of the way. Who wanted to be going to class all day? Not me!

After my eight o'clock classes, I had time before my next class for breakfast. Taylor tagged along after improv two. We met Symone in the cafeteria every Monday, Wednesday, and Friday for breakfast.

Symone was sitting at a high table with a plate of waffles and bacon. I sat my plate of eggs, sausage, toast, and pancakes on the table with a cup of grape juice. Taylor sat down with a bowl of cereal and a side of fruit with a glass of orange juice.

"Hey, y'all," said Symone.

"Morning," said Taylor.

"Hey, hey," I smiled.

Symone asked about our morning class.

"Y'all passed your commercials?"

Taylor chewed a spoonful of her cereal before answering.

"We passed. DaNia had her partner nervous. That poor girl already be panicking about life! DaNia had her about to bite off her fingers."

"Oh, yeah, you were late, that's right," said Symone.

"I want another partner. Late or not. I was gonna pass, but ole girl be stressed about all projects," I said.

Taylor then said, "I'mma start being late."

Me and Symone both looked at her. Symone took a sip of her apple juice.

"Why would you wanna be late?"

Taylor slowly turned her head toward me.

"So Professor Davenport's fine ass can wait on me!"

Symone laughed. "The man is fine, but what are you talking about?"

Taylor was still staring at me.

"Professor Davenport waited on somebody to get to class before he started," she said.

I laughed. "You jealous?" I teased.

"Hell yeah!" laughed Taylor.

We all laughed. Taylor kept going.

"He's my man!"

"Does he know that?" I asked.

"He plays hard to get, but he knows!"

Taylor then laughed at herself. She was the funny one out of us three who didn't mind saying exactly what was on her mind. Symone agreed with her.

"I have to agree with you. The man stays looking good! He doesn't even have to be all dressed up to look good!"

"He is handsome," I said.

"Handsome!" they both said.

"Yeah!" I laughed. "Handsome!"

"The man is fine!" reiterated Taylor.

"Yeah! Where did you get handsome from?" asked Symone.

I leaned back in the chair, thinking about Professor Davenport standing in front of the auditorium performing lines from a script.

"Have you really listened to him to speak? His voice is not too deep or too loud. His voice his strong and powerful, all while being sincere and warm."

I thought about his eyes. *For some reason, he always chose to connect his with mine.* I mean, I knew why I never bothered to look away. I wondered if he knew his eyes were luring me in, and it was hard for me to fight the hook, so I just stopped trying to force myself to look away. Cause every time I did, his voice tugged my spirit, my mind reacted, and my eyes were back with his.

"His eyes," I said to them. "A pretty brown. The waves in his hair! The way he walks. He is such a confident man. A confident and highly intelligent, successful black man."

Taylor waved her hand in my face. "Hello!"

I blinked my eyes and looked at her and then at Symone.

"Come back to planet Earth! Cause you clearly jetted to planet Davenport!"

Symone started laughing at how Taylor tried to use his name. I didn't find it funny. I thought it was wack!

"Yeah, you tried it," I said.

"Wait a minute," said Taylor. "You really been checking out Professor Davenport."

"He's attractive," I said. "Y'all just only pay attention to physical features. That's with every dude y'all see!"

"What's wrong with that?" laughed Taylor.

"There is more to a guy than his looks," I said.

"You're right," said Symone. "I can understand why you're saying that. You do pay attention to everything about Lil Greg."

"Yeah," I said, lowering my head and picking at the scrambled eggs with my fork.

I heard Taylor say, "Awe, man, the conversation just got serious."

"I was late because of him," I said.

"What happened?" asked Taylor.

"He was having one of his moments."

"Are you good?"

"I've been dealing with Lil Greg and his problems for a long time. I'm always okay in the end."

Taylor smiled at me. "You're a good person and woman to him, Da'Nia."

"I'm holding on," I smiled.

"One day I'mma be like you," said Symone. "I just don't see myself being dedicated to a guy right now."

"Be careful, watch what you say," I said. "Being in a relationship with a guy who has bipolar disorder isn't easy. I try to stay positive. It's hard."

"Y'all have history, too," said Symone. "I can imagine that helps you think of the good times."

"It does," I said.

Taylor looked at the time on her phone.

"I hate to leave right now, but I need to stop by the library before going to my next class."

"Okay," smiled Symone.

"I need to start heading to my class, too," I said.

Taylor stood up from the table.

"I got to make you laugh before I go," she said to me.

"What, Taylor?" I smiled.

"You got a man! Don't be worried about my boo, Jett!"

"Shut up!" I laughed.

Taylor hugged me. "You know I'm here for you if you wanna talk."

"I know. Thank you, Tay," I said, hugging her back.

"You're welcome, Nia."

I hugged Symone. "See you later."

"Aight, y'all. I'm finna go to the room and go back to sleep."

Me and Taylor laughed, walking over to the conveyor belt to place our used dishes on it. We headed in different directions when we walked out of the cafeteria.

I started on the beige path toward my class. I opened my AirPods case. I was putting the left one in my ear when I hard someone call my name. Turning my head to the right, in the direction of the voice, I saw Haze.

Haze was a junior like me. His minor was Biology Pre-Med. His minor was me! If his head wasn't in the books, it was up my behind! We met during freshman development. We had the same class. He would sit by me every day! He made it known he wanted me. I told him we could only be friends. I never went into details about my relationship with Lil Greg. Mainly because it was sensitive. Telling Haze would make me feel like I was telling Lil Greg's business. It also didn't feel right because Haze was interested in me. He wasn't the guy who could be friends with a female he was interested in and listen to her problems. *He was the type of guy who would take advantage of her vulnerability.*

He could be arrogant and somewhat selfish. Both of those made him unattractive. Physically, he was cute. He wasn't really my type, but I gave all men a chance. Haze was around 5'7. He wasn't a chocolate drop like my Lil Greg or warm caramel vanilla like Professor Davenport. He was smooth golden brown. He kept a low cut with groomed facial hair. He wasn't a small-town boy growing up. He was from Cali. That's one way we were different, and it showed. I took my time with everything. He was very demanding and pushy.

"What's up, DaNia, he said, catching up to me.

"Hey, Haze," I said, continuing to walk down the path.

"You good?" he asked me.

"I'm fine, how about you?"

"I'm straight," he said. "You headed to class?"

"Yep..."

"I'mma walk you."

"Of course, you are..."

"Why you say it like that?"

"You know why I said that."

"Naw, I don't. If I did, I wouldn't have asked."

I stopped walking. I folded my arms. He stood there in a pair of jeans and a white Polo T-shirt with a black horse.

"You could ask me, can you walk me to class."

"Ask!" he said.

"Yes!" I said, rolling my eyes.

Haze was so close-minded. Another thing that was unattractive about him.

"Why would I ask?" he asked.

I sighed. "It's sweet. Asking to walk me to class is nice and simple."

Haze shrugged his shoulders.

"I mean, I told you though."

I started walking back toward my class. I wasn't about to stand there and talk to a brick wall. He followed me like I knew he would.

"What you doing this weekend?"

I snatched myself around so quick.

"I knew it was something you wanted."

"DaNia, I've been trying to take you out for three years. You knew that was coming."

"I did! You're right! It's been three years, and you haven't learned anything. Maybe you only wanna do things your way."

"You would prefer that I ask you things instead of telling you."

"Right, but you always come out the gate wrong! Plus, I've told you we can only be friends."

"You're supposed to have a man. I've never seen you with a guy on campus!"

"Cause he's not here, duh!"

"You're always so damn mean and rude. You must not be happy."

I wanted to slap the taste out of his mouth! It wasn't that I was unhappy! I was worn out. I was holding on as best as I could. I worried about Lil Greg

THE RECIPE OF A GODLY WOMAN IX: HOPE

every second, minute, and hour! I couldn't walk away from him! I was *hoping* he would get better. I couldn't add Haze to my life to complicate things. His persistence made me think about being patient to let him grow out of his immaturity and self-centeredness.

I wanted to respond to his comment, but I decided not to. Instead, I said,

"I'm busy this weekend. Saturday, I'm volunteering with Campus Ministry. They are collecting clothes to donate to the women and children's shelter."

Haze sighed. "You're going home to church on Sunday."

"Every Sunday," I said, stopping in front of the building where my class was. Haze opened the glass door for me.

"Aight, see you around, DaNia."

"Thank you," I said, walking into the building.

He didn't come in. I didn't bother to turn around to remind him he was walking me to my class. Number one, I didn't need to. Number two, I knew he was probably upset about me turning him down.

LATOYA GETER

Haze

What did DaNia want from me? For three years, I had been trying to take her out. That's it! That's all! I wasn't even tryna smash! There were a couple of females on campus that I just wanted to hit. DaNia was on a list by herself. I was actually trying to get to know her. She said she was in a relationship. She always threw that in my face. I didn't want to hear about another dude. I wanted her, and that's all I wanted to talk about.

We were friends, but I wasn't accepting that. I wasn't gone give up. I had a feeling her relationship wasn't as good as she was acting like it was. She swore I didn't listen to her. I was going to show her that I did.

The campus ministry parking lot was packed with students. Each club, department, fraternity, organization, and sorority had a table at the Campus Ministry's clothing drive. I figured DaNia was the theatre table. I walked around the parking lot, looking for the table. I saw the comedy and tragedy masks in the colors of Ross and Stone, burgundy and orange. I headed that way. When I made it to the table, I saw DaNia was about to lift a box full of clothes.

"Let me get that for you."

DaNia turned around to see me. "Hey, Haze," she said, sliding over.

"What's up," I said, picking up the box. "I'm following you."

DaNia led me to the campus ministry building. She held the door opened for me. I walked through the door with the box. Students were moving all over the building. Some had boxes of clothes. Others had bags. Students were even carrying piles of clothes. I followed DaNia to a room. Students were putting clothes in a large bin.

"Empty it here," she said.

I emptied the box. The bin was halfway full. Me and DaNia walked out of the room and headed back to the table.

"I didn't expect to see you here," she said to me.

"Well," I said. "I want to take you out, but you said you would be here. I don't think you're gonna be here all night, but I don't want to argue with you about it. So I'm here to show you that I do listen to you."

DaNia smiled at me, nodding her head.

"What does that mean?" I asked her.

"That you listened," she said.

"So, I got some points today?" I asked her.

DaNia shook her head at me.

"I don't care how many points you wanna give yourself today. Points don't change that I'm in a relationship."

Before I knew it, my true feelings about her relationship came out.

"Whoever he is, I don't care. If we ain't talking about me and you, I don't wanna hear it."

DaNia stopped in mid-stride. She folded he arms, looking up at me. I then realized I messed up.

"It's always about you! It's been three years about you trying to get me! What about me? Have you ever thought that you make things hard for me? Have you ever thought you could complicate things for me?"

DaNia was snapping at me. I don't think she cared that other students were around. She had more to say.

"You don't have to tell me you don't care about my boyfriend! I know that! Which is another reason why I won't go out with you! You don't care about disrespecting another man."

I couldn't even say nothing. She was on my ass, and she wasn't letting up. I couldn't get a sigh out!

"Where are your clothes?" she snapped.

Clothes? I looked down at my black basketball shorts and a gray T-shirt.

"My clothes?" I asked her. "I got on clothes…"

"Not your clothes!" she snapped. "Where are the clothes you're donating?"

I made up in my mind before I got there that I was gone donate some money.

"They got Cash App or something?"

DaNia scrunched up her face. She shook her head while rolling her eyes. Well, that pissed her off even more.

"It's a clothing drive!"

"And they should be taking money. They can go buy new clothes with the money."

"The point was to bring clothes," she said, folding her arms and snatching her head to the right.

"I ain't got no clothes to give," I said. "I wear all of my clothes I got here on campus.
"There you go again, being selfish. It's a clothing drive for women and children!" snapped DaNia.
She snatched the box from me. She started walking back to her table, leaving me standing in a crowd of students moving around with clothes.

DaNia

I could see Taylor made it to our table while I was walking back. Symone walked up right when I did. I threw the box on the table. One of our female classmates picked it up.

"What's wrong with you?" asked Symone.

Taylor then said, "Yeah, throwing boxes!"

"Haze!" I snapped. "He is so selfish!"

"He's here?" asked Symone.

"Yeah," I said. "Only because I'm here."

"Of course, that's why," laughed Taylor. "That boy ain't giving up on having you."

"If I were single, he would have to work on his arrogant and selfish ways before I would think about giving him a chance."

"So, you would give him a chance?" asked Symone.

"I said, think. Technically, he is disrespecting my current relationship."

Taylor eyed me. "Can I be honest with you, DaNia?"

I was fortunate to have friends who were honest with me. Our circle didn't sugar coat anything. We lived in our truth. We may not have always liked it, but we didn't ignore the truth.

"I'm listening," I said.

THE RECIPE OF A GODLY WOMAN IX: HOPE

"You and Lil Greg aren't married. The relationship ain't the best either."

Taylor had a point. I didn't take that from her.

"Okay," I said. "I'm also not about to go out with a guy who doesn't care about my current relationship. Bad relationship or not, I'm in one."

Our classmate coming back to the table with the box stopped us from talking about my personal life. We then heard,

"Hello, ladies."

I knew the voice from anywhere. My head turned first. As always, my eyes lock with his. I couldn't find the words to speak. Taylor had it covered.

"Hey, Professor Davenport."

Professor Davenport was carrying a small pile of folded clothes. I wondered where the clothes came from. He never wore a wedding ring. They couldn't have belonged to his wife. Just because he didn't wear a wedding ring didn't mean he wasn't married.

"Hey, Miss. Reynolds," he said, handing me the clothes.

"Hi, Professor," I said, taking the clothes.

"You all been collecting a lot of donations?"

"I just got here," said Taylor, looking at me.

"Oh, yes. We have collected about ten boxes. When we fill up the box, we take them inside and put them in a larger bin."

"Great," he smiled.

More students came up with donations in bags. He moved to the side, standing next to me. The man smelled so good. I was tryna focus on taking the donations. Once the students dropped off their donations, we thanked them, and they went on their way.

A student came up to our table with a camera.

"Can I get a photo of the theatre department for the campus newspaper?"

Symone slid out of the way.

"Not my department," she laughed.

Taylor covered her face and moved to the opposite side of the table.

"I don't do pictures."

She winked at me before saying,

"DaNia and Professor Davenport can take it."

I could have punched her in the face! I didn't mind taking a picture with him, but I wasn't expecting to be in the picture with the man alone. Luckily, we were at a campus event. The picture wouldn't look bad.

I didn't move to adjust for the picture. I thought I was in the right spot. Professor Davenport clearly thought differently. He moved closer to me. The student held the camera up. He started to count. By the time he made it to three, *Professor Davenport's arm was around my waist. Shocked and surprised*, I could only smile as the camera flashed.

THE RECIPE OF A GODLY WOMAN IX: HOPE

Lil Greg

I pulled opened the glass door. The lobby area was empty. The receptionist at the desk knew me. She smiled at me.

"Hi, Greg."

"Hey," I said.

"Go on back," she said. "They're waiting for you."

I opened another door leading to a hallway. I walked down the hallway past a bathroom. A third door read, Debbie Arbor, LPC. I pushed that door open. There was a circle of four chairs. My therapist sat in one. My mama was in one. I knew one of the remaining two chairs belonged to me. I wondered where the fourth person was. I was late, and they still weren't there.

"Hey, Son." said my mama.

"Hey, Mama," I said, staring at the empty chair.

"It's good to see you, Greg," said my therapist.

I still didn't take my eyes off the chair.

"Where is he?" I asked.

Neither one of them said anything. I looked at my mother. She gave me a light smile. I turned to my therapist.

"You said he confirmed."

She ran her hand through her blonde hair.

"He did confirm, but he's not here."

"Did he call?"

"He hasn't called," she said. "We called him. We didn't get an answer."

I took out my phone from my back pocket. We didn't talk much. I still had his number. I went to my contacts, found his number, and hit the dial button. The phone rang and rang. No answer. I ended he call.

"He didn't answer."

My therapist had a suggestion.

"How about you sit with us? We can go ahead and start. If he comes, he can join us."

"I've had sessions with my mama," I said. "This was supposed to be a family session with him too."

My mama looked up at me. "Son, you know I don't mind having sessions with you. We can start."

"No!" I growled.

My therapist kept tryna get me to sit down.

"Your mother has always been so supportive. She is here. We can start with her. If we go ahead and start, we don't have to be too long."

"I know," I said. "Thank you for being here, Mama. He was supposed to be here. I ain't staying."

I went to the door and pulled the knob. I could hear my mama calling my name. I din't turn around. I was pissed. Thre was nothing she or my therapist could say that would make me stay. I pulled open the door and left the room.

THE RECIPE OF A GODLY WOMAN IX: HOPE

DaNia

Symone was sitting on her bed, typing on her laptop. I was at my desk looking over lines for my Acting III class. My phone that was sitting on the desk started to ring. I looked over to it and read it: *Bestie Bae.*

I looked at the time. He was supposed to be in a family therapy session. Why was he calling me? When the phone stopped ringing, I opened the Life 360 app. He was driving. He was headed my way. As I was about to call him back, he called me back.

"Hey," I said, answering his call.

"Babe..." he said.

"Yeah..."

"I'm on my way to see you."

"You're supposed to be in a family session."

"I left," he quickly said.

"You left," I repeated.

"Yes. I'm not going back."

"What happened?"

"I need to see you," he said, avoiding the question.

"You know I'm here for you," I said.

Normally, I would meet Lil Greg somewhere. He didn't tell me where we were meeting. Instead, he came onto the campus. He asked me to ride with him. I rode with him. He drove out to a nearby wooded area. I had passed by the area on my way back from school. I never thought to stop. I always wondered where the path that could be seen from the street led to.

We got out of his car. I started to walk down the path.

"I'm guessing your session didn't go well," I said.

"My dad didn't show up."

Lil Greg was supposed to have a family session with both of his parents. His therapist thought it would help him with coping with his childhood trauma.

"I'm sorry, babe," I said.

"I feel like when I want to start working or trying in therapy, stuff like this happens. So, what's the point?"

"You did good today. Don't give up. I know Auntie Lauren was there."

"Yeah, she was there. She wanted me to stay."

"You should have stayed and had the session with her."

"We have had so many sessions."

"I'm quite sure there is still more healing that needs to happen between you and her."

"My dad is a part of that."

"True," I said. "If he isn't willing to help or get through things with both of you and your sister, you can't make him. You have to cherish the people who are trying to get through the rough times with you. The one person who has been there for you is your mama."

Lil Greg nodded his head. We stopped in front of a small stream. I looked up at him, staring out into the water.

"I have more than my mama," he said.

I knew he was talking about me. I then looked out into the water. I thought about where the water could be coming from and how it got there. I knew where my best friend's issues were stemming from. I didn't know if he would ever get back to a steady flow like the river we both were watching. I didn't know if our flow would ever return to its original rhythm. There was once a time when we were there for one another. Our relationship was becoming me being there for him, but he wasn't there for me.

Anytime I felt like giving up, my caring and patient heart wouldn't let me. I tried my best to hold on to *my hope*. I closed my eyes, took a deep breath, and let it out.

"You do have more than your mama," I said, holding back my tears. "You have your sister."

I felt Lil Greg's arms around my waist. He stood behind me, and I leaned back into his chest.

"I have you," he said.

"Yeah," I said. "You have me."

When I spoke those words, it seemed like the stream eased its flow. It almost stood still.

LATOYA GETER

Professor Jett Davenport

My students were seated when I walked into class. I looked for Miss. Reynolds, in particular. She was sitting next to Miss. Fletcher. I was glad she was in class.

"Good morning, class," I said.

My class greeted me back. We were working on improvisations during a production. The students had scripts for plays. They were to improvise between the lines.

The second group was up performing on the stage. They weren't the strongest group in the class, but they were doing good. I scanned the class to see their reaction to the duo. *Miss. Reynolds caught my attention. She was barely up. She was nodding. Miss. Fletcher noticed I was looking their way. She nudged Miss. Reynolds. DaNia eased her head up from the palm of her hand. To see her sleeping in class was off. She was always attentive. She never slept. I kept watching her throughout the class.*

DaNia's group was the fourth group to perform. She yawned before getting up out of her seat. She moved so slow. Her outfit was off again. Another hoodie and leggings with a pair of Nikes. Her natural hair was on top of her head in a messy bun.

Her partner delivered lines first. The minute DaNia opened her mouth and delivered her lines, I

THE RECIPE OF A GODLY WOMAN IX: HOPE

knew she definitely wasn't having the best morning. Her sluggish delivery without emotions and emphasis was not her. I wanted to interrupt the performance, but I couldn't show favoritism. As much as I hated to give her a low grade for that day, I had to. Her performance was below average, but a C was all I could give her. Something was going on with her. I couldn't fail her.

DaNia

On my way to my second class for the day, I had my AirPods in my ear. "Same Grace," by William Murphy, had me thinking about my relationship with Lil Greg. Deep down, I felt he could make it out of the situation. At the same time, I knew he had to want to make it out. I had to come to terms with my feelings and reality. I wanted to help him. I wanted to continue to be there for him, but I was tired. Not only was I tired, I wasn't benefiting from the relationship. *Was I losing hope?*

I opened the glass door of the building where my class was. Haze was standing by the elevator. I didn't have time for him. I was tired. I was confused. I couldn't even roll my eyes at him. I went right for the stairs. I felt hands on my arm. I stopped at the stairs. Closing my eyes, I took my AirPods out of my ears. I turned around to him while putting them in the case.

"I gotta get to class."

"May I walk you to class?" he asked me.

He finally asked me. I squinted at him. He was up to something! He was always up to something! It was Haze! He wanted one person and one person only! Me!

"Haze, I'm in a —"

THE RECIPE OF A GODLY WOMAN IX: HOPE

"You're in a relationship," he said. "I know that. I'm gonna respect that. I'm just asking to walk my friend to class."

I sighed, staring at him. I felt like he was still trying to get me by doing what he was tired of hearing me say.

"You can walk me to class."

I started up the stairs. Haze followed behind me.

"Are they still taking donations at Campus Ministry?"

I stopped walking. I quickly turned around. Was he really going to donate clothes?

"What?" he smiled.

"You have clothes to donate?"

"I do," he said. "I called my mom and sister. They mailed a box of their clothes."

I smiled. "Really?"

Haze started up the stairs again. "Yes, I'll come back after your class. I'll have the box. We can take it over to Campus Ministry. You cool with that?"

"Yeah," I smiled, starting back up the stairs.

After my class, Haze was waiting on the first floor for me. We went out to the parking lot near the building. He let down the cab of his truck. I saw the box of clothes.

"You do have donations," I smiled.

"Yeah, I wasn't lying," he laughed.

Haze walked over to the passenger side of his truck. He opened the door for me. I hopped in the truck. He closed the door and got in on the driver's side. He drove about three blocks to Campus Ministry.

Students were there to take the donations. On our way out of the building, Haze asked me,

"Where do you like to eat?"

I laughed at his way of trying to take me out without saying just that. He was being creative. He wasn't being blatantly disrespectful.

"I'm a simple girl," I said. "Diners and homemade cooking will do me just fine."

"Diners..." he repeated as if he couldn't believe what I said.

"Yes, diners," I emphasized.

"You don't seem like a diner type of girl."

I laughed. "But I am."

"Aight," he smiled. "When are you free to have a quick bite to eat?"

I smiled, shaking my head at him.

"What?" he asked, laughing.

"You're not slick."

"I'm not tryna be. You said we're friends. I'm being a friend."

"I'm free Saturday evening."

"Is it okay if I pick you up, or do you wanna drive?"

"I'll drive," I said.

"Okay. I'll text you Saturday morning about where we'll be going."

"Alright," I smiled.

We made it back to his truck. He opened the door for me again. I hopped in. Once he got in on the driver's side, he drove me to my dorm. He stopped the truck in front of the building. Symone and Taylor were walking to the door when I opened the truck

THE RECIPE OF A GODLY WOMAN IX: HOPE

door. I hopped down, grabbing my backpack and purse.

"See you, Saturday," said Haze.

"See you then," I smiled before closing the door.

I turned around to see Symone and Taylor had stopped at the front entrance of the building. Symone had her hand on her hip, staring at me. Taylor's arms were folded. She, too, was staring me down.

"Not you getting out of Haze's truck," said Symone.

"And you're seeing him Saturday," said Taylor.

I laughed at them. "We're friends. Stop being dramatic."

"You were just mad at the man a week ago!" said Taylor.

"Right!" said Symone. "What is going on?"

I pushed past my girls. I pulled the door open to our dorm building. They followed me inside.

"Nothing is going on," I said, walking to the elevator. I pressed the up button.

"Lies," said Taylor. "Tell us!"

I laughed as the elevator door opened. We stepped on.

"He's being a better friend," I said.

"Define better!" said Taylor.

"Oh my goodness!" I laughed. "He asked to walk me to class. He got donations mailed here from his mom and sister. We took them to Campus Ministry. He asked me where I liked to eat. I told him. We're going to eat on Saturday."

"Um, hello!" said Taylor. "This is a guy who wants to be with you. Miss. I'm in a relationship!"

"He wasn't being disrespectful toward my relationship."

Symone eyed me.

"Something happened when you went to meet Lil Greg, didn't it?"

"Is that why you were sleeping in class?" asked Taylor.

"Yes, and yes," I said, lowering my head.

The elevator opened on our floor. We went to our door. Symone used her key to open the door. We walked in, and I flopped down on my bed.

"I'm tired," I said, continuing the conversation about my relationship with Lil Greg.

"What happened to you holding on?" asked Symone.

"I'm holding on, but I'm tired."

Taylor sat down at my desk.

"You know how I am. I ain't beating around no bushes. You're either done, or you're holding on by a thin string. Which one? I'm asking cause Haze has made minor changes, and you're going out with the man. Going to eat with a friend sounds good. The hell with that! You're going on a date with Haze."

Not only did I need to be honest with my friends. I had to be honest with myself.

"I'm holding on by a string," I said.

Symone came and sat by me.

"I know this is hard for you."

"It's very hard," I said. "I wanna be there for him, but his mental state is wearing me down."

"Yeah, you were sleeping in class," said Taylor. "And you bombed your improv."

"I know," I said. "I wasn't myself."

Symone rubbed my back.

"You've been dealing with this since our freshman year."

"Next year, we have to get through all our advanced classes with a B to even graduate," said Taylor. "How are you gonna get through senior advancement in a relationship like this?"

I fell back on my bed. My senior year had crossed my mind. Taylor was right. I had to be on top of my classes to pass. Meeting Lil Greg and trying to help with his problems was causing me to fall off academically.

"I honestly don't know," I said, staring at my ceiling.

"Well," said Taylor, "Being in a relationship with a guy with mental issues and entertaining a so call friend who really wants to be with you sholl ain't gone be good."

Symone looked down at me, "She's right, Nia."

"I can handle Haze," I said.

"You can't handle Lil Greg," said Taylor. "He calls, and you go running."

I sat up, rolling my eyes at her. Taylor sighed.

"Aight! My bad. Too low and too far. Didn't mean for it to sound bad, but that's the truth."

I had enough. I was done talking to them.

"I need to study," I said.

Taylor shook her head at me. "That's your way of kicking me out. Aight! Whatever. I'm finna go."

Taylor got up from my desk. She went to our dorm room door and opened it.

"Call me if y'all go to the cafe for dinner."
"Okay," said Symone.
I didn't say anything to her. I only stared out of the window next to my bed.

THE RECIPE OF A GODLY WOMAN IX: HOPE

DaNia

Saturday morning, my phone vibrated on the small dresser next to my bed. I made it through the night without a call. So, I knew Lil Greg was not texting me. I rolled over in my bed, picking the phone up from the dresser. Haze had texted me. I opened the text to see the restaurant he wanted me to meet at. I instantly got mad. The restaurant was nothing like a diner. It wasn't simple! Nothing about it said a simple down, home, feel-good restaurant. I clicked the link to the restaurant and went from being mad to pissed at the five-star seafood restaurant. I didn't even like seafood. My family loved it—especially my sisters. I didn't care for it. I really wanted to text him and tell him how I felt. Something was telling me to be nice. At least "my friend" was trying to take me out. "My boyfriend" wasn't mentally stable enough to have a conversation with me. I held onto my negative thoughts. I went ahead and texted back, telling him I would be there.

The restaurant didn't say a casual dress or jeans and a t-shirt. I had to pull out a black fitted spaghetti strapped knee-length dress with sliver open-toe shoes. I stepped out of the bathroom in the outfit. Symone, who was sitting at our desk, turned completely around.

"Girl! That dress doesn't say a bite to eat!"

"That's cause he sent Niles Shore!"

Symone laughed. "You don't even like seafood."

"Exactly!" I said. "Plus, I told him I like simple things. I don't want to go, but I'mma be nice."

"You're being nice to the spoiled, arrogant, selfish rich kid who you claim not to stand. Yeah, you're almost out of your relationship."

"Don't say that," I said.

"I'm not. Your actions are."

I picked up my keys from my dresser. Symone gave me a hug.

"Be safe. I would say enjoy yourself, but I don't know what to say."

"I don't know what to tell you to say," I said.

I then left the dorm room and headed to the restaurant. Haze was already there when I arrived. He was standing near the door, waiting for me. I looked him over. He knew what he was doing when he chose the restaurant. Him being dressed in black slacks with a dark green dress shirt and bowtie with a matching suit jacket told me so.

Haze reached out to hug me. As much as I didn't want to hug him, I hugged him back.

"You look nice," he said.

"Thank you," I smiled.

I was not too fond of his outfit, but then again, I was being nice. I gave him a compliment, too.

"So do you."

"Thank you," he said as the waitress approached us to take us to our table.

"Right this way," she said.

THE RECIPE OF A GODLY WOMAN IX: HOPE

We followed her to a table for two. Haze pulled out my chair for me. I sat and prayed there was a section on the menu that I could order from. When I found the off-the-shore section, I was relieved. My attitude wasn't gonna be that bad.

The waitress came to take our orders. I ordered the baked chicken breast over rice with broccoli. Haze ordered a lobster tail. I wasn't surprised.

After taking our orders, the waitress took our menus and headed toward the kitchen area.

"You didn't want any seafood?" he asked me.

"Don't eat it," I said.

"You should have told me," he said.

"I said a simple diner."

I looked around the dim room with chandeliers and small tables covered with black table cloths. Wine glasses sat on the unoccupied tables. Other guests in the restaurant were in formal attire.

"This is not a simple diner," I said.

"Why go to a simple diner when we can afford to eat wherever we want." said Haze.

I gave a sarcastic laugh. He was so close-minded.

"Our families can afford to eat whatever they want. Yes, we both come from wealthy families, but we are regular people. This blessed young lady believes in enjoying the simple things."

"I believe in enjoying the finer things," he said.

"Nothing is wrong with enjoying the finer things in life, but there is nothing wrong with cherishing little things. Some people aren't as fortunate as we are. They have to cherish simple moments. What if you were one of them?"

"I don't know," he said, shrugging his shoulders. He didn't even try to think about the less fortunate before he responded. "I'm not one of those people, and I've never been one."

The sad part was I believed what I was hearing. I hated that I was hearing it. I thought he was trying to make improvements. The evening was going down hill.

"You could lose everything, then what?"

"It's called a savings account. My parents have had one for years. Me and my sister are good."

"Then why are you here in school?"

"To follow the family's footsteps in the medical field. We gotta keep the fortune coming."

"Regular people want to be a doctor because they like helping others."

There he was again, shrugging his shoulders.

"Notice you said, regular people."

I shook my head at him! I was so ready to go! My phone started vibrating in my purse. I opened my purse. I picked up my phone. It read, *"Bestie Bae."* As much as I wanted to answer it, I didn't. Haze was already ruining the night. I was tryna be nice. My attitude wasn't right to talk to Lil Greg. I tossed the phone back into my purse.

I was quiet for the remainder of the dinner. Haze kept trying to talk to me. I didn't have anything else to say to him. I sat at the table and ate my dinner. I wasn't even worried about dessert. When the waitress came to the table with a check, I paid for my food. I was just that mad and ready to go! When she brought back my card and receipt, I was so glad I drove myself.

THE RECIPE OF A GODLY WOMAN IX: HOPE

I didn't have to leave with him. I took my card, opened my purse, pulled out my wallet, put away my card, tossed my receipt down in my purse, pulled out my keys, and got up from the table without saying bye to him.

While I was driving back to campus, my phone started vibrating in my purse. I didn't answer it. Haze was probably tryna call me. Maybe it was Lil Greg. I still wasn't answering it. The vibrating started right back again. I kept on driving. The more it vibrated, the more I squeezed my steering wheel. Lil Greg was going to have to wait.

I found an empty spot in the parking lot of my dorm. I pulled into the space, placing my car in park. My phone was vibrating again. I snatched my purse from the passenger seat. I basically ripped it open, pulling out my phone. *My mama was calling.*

"Hey, Mama," I said, answering my phone.

"I've been trying to call you," she said.

My mama had been calling me. I thought Lil Greg was calling. I looked at my phone for text messages. She hadn't texted me. Why not? Now she did call me ten times.

"Are you on campus?" she asked me.

I noticed how calm her voice was.

"Yeah," I responded.

"Are you in your room?"

"I just got back on campus."

"Are you by yourself?"

Her calm tone with all the questions was making me concerned.

"Mama, what's going on?'

"Please answer my question."

"I'm in my car," I said.

"Where is Symone?"

"I don't know. Mama, what is going on?"

Mama was quiet for at least a minute. I then heard her voice again.

"Lil Greg tried to kill himself. He tried to hang himself. Layla was calling him. He was supposed to meet her at the shop to help her move some things. He didn't show up. She went over to his place to check on him. She got there just in the nick of time. He hadn't died, but he almost succeeded."

"He did what?" I asked with tears taking over my vision. I had heard everything my mama said. I wasn't accepting what she was saying. The tears began to fall down my face. My back hit the car seat. I could hear my mama,

"DaNia…"

"Ma'am," I answered. Tears still managed to pass my closed eyes.

"I know you, sweetie. Please do not drive home by yourself."

"Yes, ma'am," I said.

"I love you, baby girl."

"I love you too, Mama. I'll see y'all in a little bit."

I hung up the call with my mama. My head slowly fell forward, hitting the steering wheel. Every tear I had in me fell. The one thing I feared had actually happened. I didn't answer the phone for Lil Greg, and he tried to commit suicide.

I don't know how long I cried in my car. I only know I had been crying so much that Symone noticed my blood shot red eyes when I walked into our dorm room.

She rushed out of her bed and over to me.

"Nia, what's wrong? What happened?"

"Can you please come with me? I gotta go home." I still had more tears that needed to escape my pain and regret. "Lil Greg tried to hang himself. His sister found him."

"Yeah," she said. "Let me get my shoes on."

I sat on my bed. An image of Lil Greg hanging from the ceiling came into my thoughts. My heart sank. More tears rushed down my face. I could hear Symone on the phone.

"Lil Greg tried to kill himself. We're about to head to Crestview. Okay, alright, bye."

Symone asked me if I was going to change my clothes. I was so distraught that I forgot what I was wearing. I was still in the black dress.

"Yeah," I said, getting up from the bed.

I walked over to the dresser. I pulled opened the second drawer. I could see a pair of black leggings. I slid my legs into the leggings. I could hear a knock at our dorm room door. I pulled the dress up over my head. I took a light pink t-shirt from the third drawer. Symone went to open the door. I slid into my crocs that were by my bed. I then heard Taylor ask,

"Y'all ready? I'm driving."

I turned and looked at my friends.

"Yeah, let's go."

LATOYA GETER

Audrey

The living room was quiet. My best friend sat in the middle of the couch. We had been at her house for almost an hour. She hadn't said a word. She only stared into space. I sat to her right, holding her hand. Kim was on her left. She gently rubbed her back. Allison sat next to Kim. Just as we were always there for one another, we were there for Lauren.

We heard her front door open and close. Cornelius walked into the living room. He kneeled in front of Lauren, kissing her on her cheek.

"He's going to pull through."

Lauren fell into his arms. He wrapped his arms around her. My best friend cried on her husband's shoulder.

"I've tried so hard."

Cornelius tried to calm her down.

"Baby, you have been a good, supportive mother."

"My only son. He wants to end his life. I have been watching him. I had been doing good with keeping up with him."

"Baby, don't do this to yourself," said Cornelius. "He is grown now. You can't keep your eyes on him at all times."

THE RECIPE OF A GODLY WOMAN IX: HOPE

We heard the door open a second time. I looked up to see Daniel, Will, and my brother Lemont. Daniel whispered in my ear.

"Has DaNia made it?"

I shook my head no. Daniel hugged my friends. Will hugged us as well. My brother gave me a kiss on my cheek before hugging Lauren and Kim.

"She needs to lie down," I said to Cornelius.

"No," said Lauren. "I want to go to the hospital."

"You're going to lie down," said Cornelius.

"Why? You said he is going to be fine. Why can't I go?"

"I'm not letting you go tonight," said Cornelius. "You're going to need a better mindset tomorrow. Decisions have to be made tomorrow. Layla is there right now. She needs to stay here tonight and rest. I'm not letting her stay too long. Ariel is with her right now. I got to get over to Arbrielle's to check on Cassie and tell her."

Tears fell down Lauren's face. Cornelius wiped them away. He gave her a soft kiss.

"I got you. I got us. I have our children. I promise you will go see him tomorrow."

Cornelius took Lauren's hands into his. He gently pulled her up from the couch. We heard the doorbell ring. Will went to the door to answer it. Seconds later, my baby girl walked into the living room. Her two friends from college were with her. I knew my baby had been crying. Her red, puffy eyes told me she had been crying for some time.

All of my girls had a great relationship with their aunts. Ariel and Arbrielle loved Allison. Kim was their favorite because she never held anything back from them. She wasn't afraid to get on their level to teach them a thing or two about life. DaNia was closer to Lauren before and after her relationship with Lil Greg. When she was little, she loved spending time with Lauren when she was not under me.

I wasn't surprised when she hugged me first but then fell into her aunt's arms. The two held each other tight. My eyes filled with tears, seeing my best friend and daughter share the same tears. We all knew they loved Lil Greg so much. Both of them were doing all they could to help him through the trauma. They hadn't given up on him because of his mental issues. They two of them together weren't just good for Lil Greg. They supported one another.

DaNia lifted her head from Lauren's shoulder. Lauren wiped her tears.

"Auntie, I'm sorry."

"Don't," cried Lauren. "No need for that."

"I want him to be okay," said DaNia.

Lauren assured DaNia Lil Greg would be okay.

"Your uncle made sure the best doctors are with him. Layla is there. He is going to be fine. I will be going to see him tomorrow. Get some rest. You just got in. We will start fresh tomorrow."

"Yes ma'am," said DaNia.

Lauren and DaNia shared another hug. My baby then went to her daddy. Daniel took our daughter, who was named after him, into his arms. DaNia rested her head on her father's chest. Daniel kissed her on the cheek.

THE RECIPE OF A GODLY WOMAN IX: HOPE

Before Kim and Allison left, we all shared a hug. Before I left, I made sure my best friend was upstairs, sleeping in her bed.

When Ariel and Arbrielle moved out of the nest, my husband and I had two extra guest rooms. It was no issue for DaNia's friends to stay at the house. When we made it home, I let everyone get settled in before I showered and got comfortable in my pajamas. Before going to bed, I headed to DaNia's bedroom. She and her twin brother, DJ, each had their own room. Her door was open. I peeped my head into her bedroom. DaNia was sitting in her bed typing on her laptop.

"Hey, baby girl," I said.

"Hey, Mama."

"I just came to check on you."

DaNia smiled. She reached out to me. It reminded me of when she was little and would reach for me. I knew what my daughter needed. I walked into her bedroom. I eased into bed with my baby, wrapped my arms around her, and she laid her head on my chest. I squeezed my baby tight.

"I don't know, Mama," she said. "I just don't know."

"About Lil Greg?"

"Yeah. I try so hard to be there for him. I'm so tired. It's a lot."

"Let it all out, I'm listening."

"Our relationship. I don't see it moving as long as his mental health is up and down. He doesn't do what he's supposed to do now. I can't take the risk of something happening like this when we are married with children."

"You said a lot in one statement."

My daughter looked up at me. I looked down at her and said,

"An up and down or unstable mental state now doesn't necessarily mean your relationship can't ever be."

DaNia immediately responded with, "So keep waiting?"

"I don't have to answer your question. Sounds like your mind is made up."

"My mind is telling me life could be worse in the future. My heart is reminding me that I am in love with Lil Greg. I don't want to walk away from him."

"You mentioned marriage. I didn't know you all were having those conversations."

"We haven't had one recently. We have had those conversations before."

"I want to talk to you about vows. You've heard them at your siblings' weddings. Living out vows is hard. At the wedding, you make a vow to be supportive of your partner for better, for worse, for richer, for poorer, in sickness and in health. Lil Greg is sick. Think about if you were his wife right now."

"I'm supportive," said DaNia.

"You also said you're tired," I said, reminding her of what she had just told me.

"That's normal, though, right? I'm quite sure you and Daddy have moments where you wanna throw in the towel."

"More words to describe your true feelings," I said. "Yes, your father and I get tired. We get tired of fighting the world. We stand together. We aren't perfect. Marriage is hard work. We don't get to a point where we want to throw in the towel and call it quits."

DaNia lowered her head. I said what she was struggling with admitting.

"You're not emotionally or mentally in the relationship anymore, are you?"

DaNia didn't say a word. She only shook her head no. I knew she was being honest. DaNia was very much like Ariel. You could count on them, to be honest about everything. A tear rolled down her cheek.

"I love him, Mama. I'm also scared. I don't think me being in his life is helping him. I think I'm crippling him. I'm not his girlfriend. I'm not even feeling like his best friend. I'm a crutch."

"I know Lil Greg loves you too. You're not by yourself. We all are scared. We now don't know what he will do to end his life. You can help him by supporting him. You can't make him do things. You can only cripple him if you are doing things for him."

"I answered every call except for this last one. I didn't answer, and he did the one thing I was afraid he was going to do. He tried to kill himself. When he comes to campus, I meet him where ever he is. I'm always there for him. I wasn't this time."

"You can't be available for him every second, minute, and hour. That's impossible. Tonight was an opportunity for him to use coping skills and things he learned in therapy."

"He barely goes to therapy. He doesn't always take his medicine."

"I know, your aunt has told me."

"He tells me everything. I don't know if that's a good or bad thing. He didn't tell me he was gonna try to kill himself. I didn't know the suicidal thoughts were back."

"It can be a good thing. You may not be able to help him physically, but there is one thing you can do."

DaNia looked out into space. I could tell she was thinking. I knew all my children.

"I can pray for him," she said.

"You can," I said. "The question is, have you been praying for him?"

"I haven't," said DaNia.

"But you have been worrying and trying to save him."

"Yes, ma'am."

"What should you be doing?"

DaNia sighed. "Pray for him and allow God to take care of him."

"That's it," I smiled.

DaNia nodded her head.

"Thank you, Mama."

My youngest daughter hugged me. I squeezed my baby back.

"You're welcome, baby girl."

I got out of her bed and kissed her on the cheek. I walked over to the bedroom door.

"Have a good night, DaNia."
"Goodnight, Mama," she smiled.

LATOYA GETER

Lauren

My normal Sunday morning alarm went off, although it wasn't a normal Sunday. A normal Sunday consisted of going to church with my family and having dinner at Audrey's. This Sunday, I was supposed to be heading to the hospital with my husband and daughters to make decisions about the next steps for my son.

I didn't believe in coincidences. Everything happened for a reason. My son tried to commit suicide on a Saturday. His suicide attempt had nothing to do with God. I couldn't let it be a distraction. The devil was trying to pull me away from God's word. For years, the devil was using my son as a way to pull me away from what God had for me. He wasn't successful. It made sense for him to go for the big win by trying to take my son away by suicide. My son was still alive—a huge loss for the devil. I was thankful to God. I had to give Him all the praise. I was going to church with my family. I would go to the hospital afterward.

My brother from God and pastor preached the sermon I needed. His topic was "Holding on to your faith." Helping my son battle mental illness for seven years did test my faith. There were years where I lacked an understanding of why he was suffering. I

THE RECIPE OF A GODLY WOMAN IX: HOPE

wanted to give up, but I kept my faith. In keeping my faith, I always prayed. I prayed and asked God to keep my son safe. I asked God to renew his heart, mind, and spirit. I prayed, trying to cast away the demon that was causing his issues.

While I prayed for my son, I forgot to pray for myself. I forgot to pray for strength and a will to endure. Daniel's sermon reminded me that I was a human being living in a body that would get tired, weak, and weary. Even the strong needed to give ourselves over to God to be able to fight through trials and tribulations.

A new trial was headed my way. I didn't know what would come with it. I was already giving myself, along with the entire situation, over to God.

LATOYA GETER

DaNia

Talking to my mama about my relationship with Lil Greg did help me face some feelings I couldn't face alone. I knew I had to make a decision. It wasn't a decision I felt good about. It was the best decision for me. I thought about Lil Greg as well. In my heart, it was the best decision to help him as well.

I didn't feel right going through with my final decision without talking to my Aunt Lauren. Neither one of us faced the battle alone. It was only right for me to tell her.

I did go to church the next day. I went to the main church. My heart needed a sermon from my daddy. I didn't think my auntie would be there after the night with Lil Greg, but she was there. After church, she was headed out of the sanctuary with my uncle and cousins. I caught up to her.

"Hey, Auntie."

She turned around to see me.

"Hey, DaNia," she said, giving me a hug. "We are about to head up to the hospital. Do you want to ride with us, or are your friends bringing you?"

I lowered my head. That was another thing I wanted to talk to her about. I didn't think me going to the hospital was a good idea, with or without my mind made up.

THE RECIPE OF A GODLY WOMAN IX: HOPE

I felt my auntie's finger under my chin. She lifted her finger, and my head followed. Her looking into my eyes made me tear up.

"Do we need to talk?" she asked me.

"Yes, ma'am," I said.

"Okay," she said. "You want to stop by the house?"

"I can," I said.

"Okay. I'll meet you there," she said.

My mama drove me over to my Auntie's house after church. She felt I needed to talk to my auntie alone. She dropped me off, and I headed to the front door. My aunt opened the door for me. I followed her into the backyard. We sat in two black lounging chairs on her patio. A small table sat between us. I went ahead and started to deliver the news.

"I don't think I should go to the hospital," I said.

"I agree," said Auntie Lauren.

I immediately turned my head toward her. I wasn't expecting her to agree with me. Her response shocked me.

"Your eyes told me earlier how you're feeling. You've let go."

"Auntie, I don't want to. I really don't-"

"Stop," said my Auntie, taking my hand. "It's okay to let go."

"Then why do I feel bad?"

"You have been dealing with the situation to the point where you are so used to being there for him. It has become your life. You've been in my son's life since you all were toddlers. You have been in a relationship with him since you were fifteen years old.

You're twenty-two. I know he calls you and comes to the campus. I don't need to know how you feel about dropping everything and coming to his rescue. Again, your eyes told me your true feelings."

"My life has revolved around him. I do put aside my feelings and things that I'm going through for him."

"That's not how a relationship works. He can be down, but at some point, he is supposed to support you just as you have supported him."

My auntie smiled at me. She patted the top of my hand.

"As much as I wanted you to be my daughter-in-law one day, I can't expect you to continue to live your life like this. You're young. You deserve to be happy. You aren't happy. I know you're not. I want you to be happy."

"Auntie, I can't go to the hospital and tell him we're done. That wouldn't be good for his mental state."

"You don't need to go to the hospital. It wouldn't be good for you either. You love my son, but you can't be with him. That's hard to deal with now. It's going to be very hard once you start to move forward. We're not going to add any more things to your plate of emotions."

"He is not mentally well, but he needs to know."

"You're right," said Auntie, beginning to think of a plan. "Once he is stable, we will tell him then."

"Okay…"

THE RECIPE OF A GODLY WOMAN IX: HOPE

"You live your life," she said. "We don't know what is about to happen. That shouldn't stop you from living your life."

"Yes, ma'am", I smiled. "Thank you for listening."

"You're welcome, niecey."

My aunt Lauren stood up. I looked up at her, "Auntie…"

"What's up, baby? Something else you wanna talk about?"

"I need to say something?"

My auntie sat back down. I couldn't look away from her. I wanted her to know how sincere I was.

"We have been in this together for so long. I hate to leave you to face this alone. I'm sorry, Auntie."

My auntie hugged me.

"Oh, sweetie, I won't be alone. God has already worked everything out. Promise me one thing?"

"What's that?"

"That you won't ever apologize again for putting yourself first."

I lowered my head, but she didn't let it fall too far. Her finger was under my chin again. I lifted my head.

"I promise, Auntie."

We both stood up together.

"I love you," she said, giving me one more hug.

"I love you too," I said, embracing our bond.

****

I needed time to myself. I couldn't stay in Crestview long. I had to go back to school. Midterms were coming up. I decided to stay home on Sunday and Monday. My friends left for school on

Sunday evening. My parents would be taking me back on Monday evening. Once I emailed my professors on Sunday evening, I went into my room and sat on my bed, listening to music. I tried not to think about Lil Greg, but I did. My auntie and family had gone to see him. I knew he had probably asked where I was. I hoped my aunt was able to tell him something that would ease his mind. He hadn't called me. I figured he wasn't allowed to have his phone, or maybe it was still at his place. I was relieved either way. I was barely able to think about moving on without him. There was no way I could talk to him. Talking to him would have meant telling him the truth. The truth was, we were over. The truth hurt, and I was feeling every piece of it. I loved him, but I had to let go.

Professor Jett Davenport

Monday was back before I knew it. I stopped by my office every morning before my class with my coffee in one hand and my briefcase in the other. I managed to pull open my office door. I hit the light switch on the wall. I sat my coffee down on my desk before sitting in front of my computer. I sat my briefcase on the side of my coffee. I turned on my computer. The first thing I did was check my email. There was an email from Miss. DaNia Reynolds. I opened the email, and it read,

Hello Professor Davenport,

I will be out of class on Monday. I will return on Wednesday. I do not have an excuse. I'm okay with just taking an unexcused absence.

Thank you,

DaNia Reynolds.

She wasn't turning in an excuse. I wondered why she was out. I tried to figure out why she was missing class. I thought back to the times when she was in class. She was late, sleepy, and sluggish. I thought about her. Was she going through something? Was she sick? I didn't know what was going on with her, but I planned to talk to her once she got back.

She did miss Monday, but she was back in class on Wednesday. I wrapped up the class. Students were gathering up their things to leave. I saw her putting her backpack on. I had to catch her before she left.

"Miss Reynolds," I said, calling her name.

She looked up, and our eyes connected.

"May I speak with you?"

She moved through the auditorium seats, walking down to the podium where I stood.

"Yes, Professor?"

"Do you have time to come with me to my office?"

"Um, sure," she smiled.

I could see Miss. Fletcher was waiting at the doors in the back of the auditorium. DaNia looked back at her.

"I'll catch you later."

"Alright," she smiled. "See ya later, Professor."

"Have a good day, Miss. Fletcher."

I placed all my things in my briefcase. DaNia and I headed for the side door that led to the lobby of the fine arts building. I opened the door for her, and she walked through the doorway. I followed behind her.

"How are your other classes?" I asked her.

"I'm doing good in those," she said.

"I know you're performing well. I meant the structure and challenge."

"I don't want to make it seem like the other instructors aren't good or that they aren't doing good."

"Oh no! I'm not asking for that reason. I'm asking because I've been selected to serve on our department's board of instructors. We are gathering feedback from students on how to improve the program."

DaNia smiled. "I don't know if I should say congratulations or not. It sounds like it's a big thing."

"Thank you," I said. "Only five of us were selected out of the department. I'm also the president of the board. I guess you can say it's a big deal."

I laughed a little, and so did she.

"Since you threw president in there, it's a big thing. I'm not surprised you're in that position."

"Why not?"

"Professor, you are the best instructor we have. Every student in the department knows that."

"Thank you again." I smiled.

"You're welcome. So, to answer your question, I'll say all instructors aren't you. I don't expect them to be either, but your classes are interactive, and we actually learn things that we are going to use in the industry."

"Does that mean you feel other classes aren't preparing you for the industry?"

"I'm not going to say…"

"I asked our elite student in the department for an answer."

She laughed and said, "There you go with that. I'm not the best student the department has had."

"I love how humble you are," I said. "But yes, ma'am, you are."

DaNia kept laughing. She stopped at the glass door of the building where my office was located.

"I'm not gonna keep talking about that."

She looked up at me and said,

"Just know that I pay attention to you."

I must have heard her wrong. I didn't want to ask her to repeat herself. I was too afraid I heard her correctly.

"You pay attention to me…"

Our eyes were locked again. She was the one who decided to ease out of the mesmerizing moment.

"The way you teach. I pay attention to the way you teach."

Maybe that's what she meant. There was only one way to find out.

"I've been paying attention to you, too," I said.

DaNia's eyes were back locked with mine.

"You pay attention to me…"

She heard me right. I pulled the same response she did.

"The way you perform. The way you perform in class is what I meant."

I let that simmer with her. I opened the glass door. She walked into the building. We took the elevator to the third floor, where offices were. We walked down to a suite of offices. I pulled my door open for her. She walked in, and so did I. Closing the door behind us, I watched her sit down in a chair in front of my desk. I sat on the other side. I started the conversation with,

"I've been noticing somethings. I want to help you with whatever you have going on."

THE RECIPE OF A GODLY WOMAN IX: HOPE

"What have you noticed?"

"You have been late, sleeping in class, and then you missed class."

DaNia looked away.

"From this point on, it won't happen again. None of it will," she said.

"Are you sure?" I asked her.

"Yes. At first, I was dealing with some issues, but they all have been taken care of."

I accepted what she told me. My mind drifted to the absence where she was unable to submit documentation to be excused.

"You're unexcused absence. You couldn't get an excuse. Why not? I hated to give you an unexcused absence."

"I was dealing with an issue at home. It had nothing to do with an immediate family member, so that's why I didn't have an excuse."

I appreciated her honesty. She could have lied to me. Her transparency made me want to know what was going on. I also didn't want to pressure her into talking.

"We have mid-terms coming up," I said. "Are you confident that you're going to pass with what is going on at home?" I'm only asking because you are a great student. We need your grades to remain solid."

"I will pass," she smiled.

I gave her a head nod with a smile. "Alright. Do I need to check with your instructors?"

She laughed. "I'm not ten, Professor. I communicate with them as well. I will pass their mid-terms."

"That's what I like to hear," I said, standing up.

"That's all you wanted to talk about?" she asked.

My eyes instantly connected with hers. She hurried and looked away. I eased back down into my chair.

"I'm here to listen to whatever you need to release."

DaNia's eyes made their way back over to mine. She took a deep breath before slowly exhaling.

"Professor, I'm going through a difficult time right now. I'm not quite ready to talk about it with people outside of my family and friends."

I respected and understood where she was coming from. I still felt the need to be there for her. All of my students had my office number. None of them had my personal cell number.

"You can have my number. Feel free to call or text me if you need anything."

To my surprise, DaNia didn't fight me or make an excuse as to why she couldn't take my number. She took her phone from her purse, handing it to me across my desk. I took it from her and put my number in her phone. I handed her phone back to her.

"Thank you, Professor," she said.

"Call me anytime," I smiled.

She stood up from my desk. I walked her to my office door. I opened it for her. She left my office. I wanted to watch her walk down the hallway. Instead, I closed my office door, leaned against it, shutting my eyes, thinking about her walking down the hallway.

THE RECIPE OF A GODLY WOMAN IX: HOPE

DaNia

I opened the door to the building that led to my second class of the day. Haze was standing at the stairs. Our forced dinner date came to mind. I instantly got mad.

I didn't want to talk to him. There was no way I could avoid him. Taking the elevator was not an option. I would have had to ride it with him. If I took the stairs, he was gonna follow me. I went with the stairs. He stood in front of them to keep me from going up. Childish!

"I haven't heard from you," he said. "Sunday, I texted you. Monday, you were MIA. Yesterday, I texted you. You didn't text back."

"Don't act like you don't know why," I said.

"I thought our dinner was nice."

"It wasn't!" I snapped. "It was not a simple diner or restaurant. You picked a five-star restaurant to force me to dress up like we were going on a date. I came even though I didn't want to. You made it worse! You and your close-minded mentality! My weekend started off terribly because of you! It didn't get any better after that! I didn't text or call you back because my boyfriend tried to commit suicide!"

Everything came out. I couldn't control my emotions. I was pissed at him and struggling with my decision to end my relationship with Lil Greg.

"Commit suicide..." Haze repeated.

"Yes," I said, looking away.

"I'm sorry to hear that," said Haze. "Even thought I wish things could be different between us, I can put my feelings aside and say I'm sorry. Is he doing better?"

"I don't know," I said. "We're not together anymore."

"Oh," said Haze. "You're dealing with that too, huh?"

"Yes," I said. "The last thing I need is you trying to push your way in now that you know."

"I won't do that. You were faithful to him. I know how much you cared about him."

"I still care," I said. "I love him."

Hazed lowered his head. That's not what he wanted to hear, but he knew I was always honest with him. He raised his head.

"Look, I apologize about the dinner. I'm sorry about what happened with your ex. My feelings are still the same. I'll put those aside right now, but they aren't changing."

Haze drained me! In the worst way. I still appreciated his honesty. His honesty did not make up for his rich, entitled mentality. That part of his personality was something I couldn't ignore.

I couldn't even accept his apology. "Yeah, thanks," I said, brushing past him and up the steps to my class.

Professor Jett Davenport

DaNia said she was going to pass her mid-terms. My mid-terms were improving an entire scene solo. Students were given a situation. They had ten minutes to look over their situation. Each of them was given two minutes to act out their situation. She was the second to the last student to go. I was looking forward to her performance. She walked onto the stage. She was her normal self. She was dressed in a nude sweater dress with dark brown leggings and even darker brown knee-high boots. Her hair hung down in loose natural curls that came to her shoulders.

I moved to the edge of my seat. *Of course, I knew what each situation was about. I didn't know which one she chose.*

DaNia started her scene with a light pace as if she was thinking. I still didn't know which one she chose. She said her first line.

"He knows."

She kept the light pace.

"He doesn't know."

She stopped in the middle of the stage.

"Wait. Do I really know?"

She went back to the slow pace.

"What if we both know? Then again, we both may not know. We both could be wrong. Either way, neither of us know. We won't know until we confess. Confess our attraction to one another. Confess our longing to do so. Confess what our hearts desire. Confess what our souls are missing. One another. If we confess, are we starting our path to love? Will the journey be an ease, or will we be displeased? Neither one of us will know. One of us has to allow our true feelings to show. As for me, I'll wait. Patience is a virtue, and one day, love will be my reward."

The classed clapped. I leaned back in the chair, staring at her. *She looked up, and our eyes connected. She didn't look away as she always did before. Her eyes stayed locked to mine. At that moment, I realized she chose the situation of a woman being confused about her feelings for a man. Yes, I slid the scene into the folder on purpose. I felt she would choose it, but I wasn't sure.*

She chose it and performed it so well that I was convinced but still unsure. Plus, she was my student. I would be venturing into uncharted waters. This time, it was me who eased out of our infamous eye gaze. I looked down at the roster in front of me. I marked a one hundred percent by her name for passing her midterm in my class.

DaNia

I told Professor Davenport I was gonna pass my mid-terms, and I did. I passed all five of them. My semester was back looking good. For winter break, I went back home to Crestview. Haze was constantly calling and texting me. I didn't call him back, but I would sometimes text him back.

Lil Greg was in treatment. Being back home reminded me every day. I wanted to visit him, but me showing up wouldn't help me or him. Dealing with knowing he was in treatment and being unable to see him was not helping my mood.

After winter break, I went back to school totally focused on finishing the semester. Haze and I talked. I stopped being hard on him. He could mess up my mood if I saw him. I couldn't keep arguing with the boy. He knew where I stood. He kept trying to be with me, but I only focused on school. I didn't go out with him. He only saw me on campus. I was not budging. Even when he tried to be slick, I still came with a no. A hard no!

Summer break came fast. I started my break off good. I passed all of my classes. My cumulative grade point average was still a 4.0. That's right! I never had a B on my transcript. My mama was the first generation college graduate who held onto a 4.0 all four years. I was right behind her.

The Crestview summer program was still being held at my sister's art gallery and museum. I loved to volunteer there in the summer with my family. I ran the theatre troupe. At the beginning of the program, kids could sign up to participate. I would help them learn the basics of theatre. We would also perform a short play at the end of the summer.

I was sitting on the stage searching on my laptop for things to order for the set of the play. I heard a door open. I looked over to my right to see my big sister, Ariel.

"Hey, baby sis," she said, sitting next to me and giving me a hug.

"Hey," I said, leaning into her embrace.

"How did your day go with the troupe?"

"They had a good day," I smiled. "I'm actually finding stuff for their play."

"Oh, okay. Yeah, make sure you get the list to me so I can get that paid for."

"I will," I smiled.

My sister then asked me,

"How have you been? I've watched you bounce around here with the kids, but it's almost like you're trying too hard."

My sister was right. I was doing all that I could to keep my mind off Lil Greg. The summer camp was helping, but in my down time, I still thought about him.

"I'm maintaining," I said to her. "Being here is helping."

THE RECIPE OF A GODLY WOMAN IX: HOPE

"Yeah, but we end before you go back to school. You're going to have at least a month and a half left. What are you going to do to help you keep your mind stable until you go back to school?"

"I don't know," I said.

"Why didn't you do an internship this summer?

"They aren't required."

"So!" said Ariel. "When did you start doing the bare minimum? Get the experience."

"I've never done the bare minimum. Students do them in our department. I've probably missed out."

"Summer school is in. You can still call and see if anything is available."

"The summer is almost over. I don't think anything is available. I should have done one at the beginning."

"You don't know that. There may be some program for three or four weeks. Not just an internship."

I stared into space, thinking about what I was going to do. I remembered I had Professor Davenport's number.

"I can call Professor Davenport."

"One of your instructors?"

"Yeah. He's on some board for instructors. He may be able to connect me with someone."

"I say give him a call," said Ariel. She stood up from the stage, giving me a hug.

"I gotta run and check on your nephews and niece."

"Alright," I smiled.

"Let me know about the internship or whatever, and get that list to me."

"I'm on both," I said as my big sister headed toward the side door of the auditorium.

I took my phone out of my back pocket. I scrolled through my contacts. I noticed Professor Davenport saved his name as Jett in my phone. That was unexpected, but I guess it was okay. I went ahead and called him. He answered on the third ring.

"This is Jett Davenport."

"Hey, Professor," I said.

Before I could tell him who I was, he said,

"Hey, Miss. Reynolds."

"Yeah, it's me," I said.

"Of course, it is. I recognized your voice. How are you? How has your summer break been?"

"I'm okay," I said. "About my summer break, that's why I'm reaching out to you."

"What can I do for you?"

"I know it's late for an internship. I still wanted to reach out to see if you knew of a program or something I could do. Right now, I'm over the theatre troupe at a summer program. We have a play coming up. After the summer program is over in about four weeks, I will still have the end of our summer break. I don't have anything planned."

"Back up, back up," said Professor Davenport. "You work with a theatre troupe."

"Yes," I laughed. "My family helps with a summer program—."

"The summer program your dad started in Crestview years ago."

THE RECIPE OF A GODLY WOMAN IX: HOPE

"Yes. We added the theatre troupe a year ago. After I finished my freshman year, the summer after, my family let me join the project."

"That's awesome. You're directing the play?"

"I am. I practice with the kids and get the set ready. This is my second summer doing the play."

"I have to come see the play."

My heart started to beat fast. I didn't know what to say. I didn't need this man coming to Crestview. I sure didn't need him coming to the play. Professor Davenport always came with a surprise that confused me. Yeah, I was attracted to him, but I didn't know for sure if he was attracted to me. First, it was pulling me close in the picture. Then, the talk in his office almost had me pouring out my feelings. I held it together. The situation I had to improvise in his class was not there by accident. I didn't know what he was gonna pull if he came to Crestview.

"Um, I'll text you the dates."

"Do that," he said. "I didn't know you were interested in directing as well."

"My goal is to become an actress. I do the plays for the kids."

"I think you should be versatile—more job opportunities in the future. I'm going to check my network and see what I can do for you for the rest of the summer. Internships are gone, but let me ask around, and I'll get back to you."

"You're right," I said. "It wouldn't hurt for me to keep directing and acting once I graduate. Thank you again."

"You're welcome. Don't forget to send me the dates for the play."

"I won't forget. Thank you, Professor, for your help," I said, ending our call.

THE RECIPE OF A GODLY WOMAN IX: HOPE

Professor Jett Davenport

Like all administrators, staff, and instructors at Ross and Stone, I knew about Daniel Reynolds and his family's work in Crestview. The small town was now a growing city of continued progress. I had read articles and watched videos, but I hadn't been to Crestview.

When DaNia sent me the dates, I figured spending a week in the city would be good. I could see the progress the family was making. I thought about telling her how I was interested in her, but that thought quickly left me. She probably wasn't interested in me. I thought she was. DaNia wasn't easy to read. Although she didn't pull away from at the community service event when we took the picture, threw a lil hint in my office, acted out the scene I purposely picked, and invited me to the play, I still wasn't sure.

I drove into Crestview. The three-hour drive south of the city wasn't bad. I drove an hour every day to Ross and Stone. I was used to driving two hours a day. Adding an hour didn't hurt. I lived in Addonsdale. Like Crestview, Addonsdale had the good, the bad, and the outskirts. I lived in the country parts. So when I drove past the "Welcome to Crestview" sign, I felt at home. Driving through the country outskirts made me smile. I loved to see the large fields and the cows grazing. I let the top down on my chrome Audi S5 Convertible. I cruised my way into the west side of Crestview. I drove into the parking lot of Wilmar Condos and Suites. I drove up to the front door for the valet to park my car. I got out of the car in a pair of khaki shorts and a red t-shirt with red and white Air Jordan 11 retro kicks. I took my suitcase out of the back seat. I headed inside to check-in.

Once I got to my room, I shot DaNia a text telling her I made it in. I asked her about some good places to eat. She sent me an Italian restaurant, The West Side Café and Parkston Grill. I looked up the places. The West Side Café had good reviews. I went ahead and went there.

My plan was to get my food to go. I stood in the café looking up at the menu.

"The blueberry tea is good with whatever you order," I heard her say.

I turned around to see DaNia. She was looking good in the baby blue fitted cotton long summer sundress.

"Hey, Miss. Reynolds," I said, leaning in for a hug.

"Good to see you, Professor," she said, leaning in and accepting my hug.

"How did you know I would choose this spot?"

"Everyone knows it's the best place to eat in town. I know you saw those reviews online."

"I did," I laughed.

"You're gonna see," she said. "What are you thinking about ordering?"

"It's a lot to choose from," I said, looking up at the menu.

She laughed. "Yep! It's all good too. What do you have a taste for?"

I slowly looked over at her. She smiled.

"How about you order me the best thing on the menu."

"Alrighty," she said. She walked up to the counter.

"Hey, DaNia," said the man behind the counter.

"What's up, JT? Let me get the Crestview Chicken Philly fully loaded."

"Gotcha!" he said.

"And a large blueberry tea."

"Cool. Aight. That will be fourteen eighty-five."

I took out my wallet. As I was pulling out my card to pay for the food, I saw DaNia hadn't ordered anything for herself.

"You gone get you something?" I asked her.

"I'll take a Crestview Philly fully loaded," she said.

"Add that?" asked TJ.

"Yes," I said.

"And another blueberry tea," smiled DaNia.

"Whatever she wants," I laughed.

TJ laughed. "You dining in or taking out?"

DaNia looked up at me.

"I had planned to take out, but since you're here now, I'll dine in."

"You can do takeout," she smiled.

There she was again! Confusing me! How was she going to show up at the café and then tell me to take it out?

"Let's eat in," I said.

"Alright," she smiled.

We found an empty booth. She slid in, sitting across from me.

"How was your drive in?" she asked me.

"Good and relaxing. I feel right at home here."

"I've never been to Addonsdale," she said. "We always fly out. I've never been pass Ross and Stone."

"It's not very different from Crestview. Both cities are growing every day. I live on the country outskirts."

"Country outskirts," she repeated.

"Yes," I laughed. "You're a small-town girl."

"Small-town girl," she emphasized. "Not a country girl."

I laughed. "Same thing!"

"No!" she laughed.

"I passed by farms on the way in. You mean to tell me you've never been on one one?"

DaNia cocked her head to the side. "No! I told you a small-town girl is not the same as a country girl! My older sister loves nature. My mama loves animals. That's their lane. Not mine."

The girl kept me laughing. "Farms are not bad."

"I didn't say they were. They are just not for me."

"You haven't been on one. How would you know?"

"How would you know it is for me?" asked DaNia, laughing with a neck roll.

"You could visit a farm one day."

DaNia squinted at me. She pushed her lips out with a sigh. She licked them and bit her bottom lip before letting it go.

THE RECIPE OF A GODLY WOMAN IX: HOPE

"Do you have a farm or something?"

"I do," I said.

"Woah!" laughed DaNia. "Nuh-uh! Stop lying, Professor."

"I do have a farm," I laughed.

"No way!" she laughed. "How? You're too smooth and chill. I never would have guessed!"

"I'm a farmer," I laughed. "The farm is our family business. My family provides produce for Addonsdale. I farm on the weekends. My parents had been farming since I could remember. My dad wanted me to farm full-time when I graduated high school. Farming wasn't something I saw myself doing every day. I wanted to be an actor."

"Farming and acting are two different things," she said. "How did you get into acting?"

"School," I said. "At first, we didn't have a drama class. We got the class in my sophomore year of high school. I took the class because one of my teachers said I talked too much."

DaNia laughed. "I took drama in high school, too."

"I ended up liking the class," I said. "I took Drama II my junior year and Drama III my senior year. My dad wasn't too happy when I left for college to major in theatre. After I graduated, I had some major roles in plays. I still had farming in my heart. I would send money home to help sustain the farm."

"You still helped your family out. That's amazing," said DaNia. "How did you get to Ross and Stone?"

"I had to come off the road from acting. My father passed away. My older brother isn't reliable. My family needed my help with the farm. I mainly help with the upkeep, managing, and finances. My younger brothers run the farm.

"I'm sorry to hear about your father," she said.

"Thank you," I smiled. "The farm has always been my mother's main source of income. So we had to keep it going."

"We? As in your siblings?"

"Yes. I have four brothers. I am the second born of five boys. My three younger brothers farm and hire people to work in the distribution warehouse."

"So would you say your family has made a difference in Addonsdale?"

"Most definitely," I answered. "We help residents of the city with food. Fresh food. Our farm has provided people with jobs."

"I like that," smiled DaNia.

The waitress brought our food to the table. My loaded chicken Philly looked good. I couldn't wait to taste it.

"You wanna bless the food?" asked DaNia.

"No problem," I smiled.

After I blessed our food, I picked up the chicken Philly and took a bite. It was delicious!

"Oh yeah! This is hitting!"

DaNia smiled while cutting her Philly in half.

"It's good, ain't it!"

"Better than good!"

I chewed my food before asking her,

"How does it feel to be a part of the most prominent family in Crestview?"

"Being the baby girl isn't easy when you have Ariel and Arbrielle Reynolds as your older sisters. One is almost perfect, while the other has made huge, drastic decisions that weren't good, but she fixed them. I'm left, and I know people are trying to figure me out. Daddy and Malachi being in ministry isn't bad. I'm finding my way. Mama helps me. I love people. I love giving back. So I'm good at that. I go to school and church and try to stay out of the way."

I was surprised to hear her say she was trying to stay out of the way. I had to pick her brain some more.

"You're going to be an actress. You're going to be in the entertainment business. Similar to your sister. How are you going to stay out of the way?"

"I can be an actress and not be involved in negativity."

"What about roles?"

"I don't have to choose every role that comes my way."

"True," I said. "What if it's one that could expand your career but goes against your beliefs and morals?"

DaNia didn't hesitate to say, "Depends on the message that is being conveyed."

"You're on to something," I smiled. "That fits you. I can see you taking that approach. Are you the first actress in your family?"

"I am," she smiled.

"What influenced you to become an actress?"

She gave a light laugh. "Vacation Bible School, Easter plays, Black History programs, and Christmas plays at church. I was always in a play or on a program or had a speaking part."

"Now you're putting on plays," I smiled.

"This is just my second one," she said.

"I'm sure you've put everything together like a vet in the game."

"You'll see," she smiled.

"I will," I said. "I'm ready!"

I walked her to her car after we ate. She stood outside of her car, leaning against the driver's door.

"Thank you again, Professor."

"You're welcome," I said.

DaNia opened her car door and eased in. I closed her door with ease. I waved at her as she backed out of the parking spot.

THE RECIPE OF A GODLY WOMAN IX: HOPE

DaNia

I walked into my room from a shower. My phone was my bed. I noticed I had a missed call from Haze. I really didn't want to call him back, but I did anyway. He didn't even allow the phone to ring before he picked up.

"Hey, DaNia."
"Hi, Haze."
What you up to?"
"Nothing much. About to lay down."
"Long day?"
"Yes. I've been working with my theatre troupe."
"Theatre troupe?"
"Yeah, I work with kids in the summer. We have a play coming up."
"Why didn't you tell me?"
"I don't know."
"When is it?"
"Friday."
"It's two days. I can catch a flight."
"It's not that serious," I said to him.
"It is," he said. "Plus, it's your play, right?"

"I'm directing."

"Well, yeah, I want to come support you. I get to see yo city too."

"It's so last minute."

I was trying to say anything I could to keep Haze away. I knew if he came, he would go overboard. I didn't want him to do anything in front of Professor Davenport. Neither one of us had told each other how we felt about one another, but I felt like something was there. *Our conversation at the West Side Café didn't give professor-to-student vibes. I felt like he was tryna get to know me.*

Haze hit me with, "I'm not doing anything. Could you send me the address? I'll be there."

I got quiet on the phone. He was not playing. He wasn't giving up. He was coming to Crestview.

I heard him call my name. "Da'Nia."

"Yeah, I'm here," I said.

"You gone send me the address?"

"I will," I said.

Audrey

The kids in the summer theatre troupe did a fantastic job with our second annual summer program production. I knew DaNia worked very hard, and it showed. The kids were polished with their dancing and on-stage movements. They were outspoken when delivering lines. Most of all, I was happy to see them so excited on stage. They were having the best times of their lives. I was so proud of my baby girl for giving kids in our community an opportunity to shine.

I was standing with my husband and family, waiting for DaNia to come from backstage. A man dressed in a black suit with a blue dress shirt and a dark blue tie was walking toward the stage. DaNia came through the side door of the banquet room. She spotted the man and walked over to him. I could see she was talking to the man. She was smiling. He leaned in, giving her a hug. She hugged him back, which told me she knew who he was. Out of nowhere, a young man joined the duo. Where did he come from? He had a bouquet of different types of flowers. I saw my baby's face drop. She stared at the young man. She was hesitant about taking the bouquet, but she took it. Now, I did raise my children to be polite. I watched my girl tell the young man thank you. I noticed that she didn't hug him like she hugged the man.

Both of the men were obviously there for her. Kids and parents were all over the place. Neither one of them joined a family. I nudged my husband, slid my arm under his, and made my way to the trio. I was practically dragging Daniel at first. Finally, he picked up on what was going on.

"Good evening," I said as we approached them.

The man and the young man turned our way. I made sure to make eye contact with the young man. He appeared to be closer to DaNia's age. The flowers gave away his motive. He needed to know who we were. Yes, my husband and I still stayed out of our kids' relationships, but DaNia was too close to graduation to have *another* distraction.

DaNia introduced everyone.

"Daddy, Mama, this is Haze. Haze, meet my parents, Reverend Daniel Reynolds and Mrs. Audrey Reynolds."

My husband shook the young man's hand. I shook his hand afterward. DaNia introduced the man. I shook his hand. Professor Davenport or something similar was his name, one of her instructors. I missed some of the introduction. I was too busy focusing on the young man. I had some questions for DaNia. She never told me another young man was in the picture.

That night, I walked down the hallway of our home and into DaNia's room. She was sitting on her bed, scrolling through her phone.

"Hey, Mama," she said to me.

THE RECIPE OF A GODLY WOMAN IX: HOPE

"Hey, baby girl," I said, walking into her room. I sat down on the edge of her bed.

"Haze," I said.

DaNia didn't say a word. Her face was blank.

"I saw you at the play and how you interacted with him."

"He is barely a friend," she said.

"Does he know that?" I asked her. "The young man had flowers for you. He must think otherwise."

"He wishes we were together."

"I mean, you just got out of a relationship–."

DaNia hurried and got the point for me.

"He has been trying to get with me. Since my freshman year, I've told him we can only be friends. I told him I was in a relationship. He knows I'm single now, but we are only friends."

"He's been persistent…"

DaNia rolled her eyes.

"Mama, you don't know Haze. He's arrogant and a spoiled rich kid. He is selfish. He is simple-minded. We don't click."

"You really aren't interested in him."

"No, Mama, I'm not."

I raised my hands, surrendering the topic.

"Alright, I'll leave it alone. I was checking because he seems to be very interested in you."

"Thanks, Mama," she said. "You have nothing to worry about. Trust me."

"I trust you," I said. "I know you're going to stay focused and finish your degree."

I kissed my daughter on her cheek before leaving her room.

LATOYA GETER

DaNia

I was on a Facetime call with Taylor and Symone. I was telling them how Haze showed up to play with flowers. I left out the part about Professor Davenport being there. I still wasn't sure about what was happening between us. I didn't want to speak too soon. I also didn't want to speak on something that could actually be nothing at all.

A call was coming in from him. I only told my friends I would call them back. I hurried off the phone. I didn't want them asking any kinds of questions.

"Hello," I answered.

"Hey, Miss. Reynolds," he said.

"Hey, Professor!"

"I have some news for you."

"About an internship?"

"Well, it's not actually an internship, but you can get experience. I enjoyed the play. You did a good with the kids in your community. I immediately thought about a previous student of mine. He is a director. He has a play that he is traveling with. His next stop is Atlanta. He will be there for a week. I think it would be good for you to go there and work with him. His name is Andrew Phillips. He is known as Drew Phillips."

I had heard of him. He was known for black religious comedy productions.

"I've heard of him."

"Have you watched any of his plays?"

"No," I said. "I'm willing to go, especially since you took time out to find it for me at the last minute. On the account that I waited so late."

"Good. Don't worry about all of that. You're going. That's all that matters."

"Wait, since this is not an internship, Ross and Stone won't cover any expenses. So, I'll need to talk to my parents about a flight and hotel."

Professor Davenport then said,

"Your hotel, flight, and meals will be paid for. The only thing I need you to do is find a flight that is good for you. The play begins on August first. I would like for you to be there at least a day early to meet Drew."

I was wondering how my hotel, flight, and meals were being paid for if Ross and Stone weren't paying. Plus, he didn't know Daniel and Audrey. Even though I was grown, I still lived in their house. They were going to want to know everything. My mama had to know where I was. I almost wanted to take her with me. I had only been to college without my mama, and I was home every weekend to see my girl.

"My parents are going to want to know. I have to tell them."

"No problem," he said. "You will be staying at the Candler Hotel. Once you get your flight, the hotel will be booked."

"Any flight?"

"Any flight is fine."

"We fly first class over here."

He laughed. "That's the only way I fly."

I had to ask the question! I had a feeling he was up to something. If Ross and Stone weren't paying for a first-class flight, then who was?

"Professor, who is paying for this?"

He laughed again. "The board has funds that we can use for students."

My heart kinda fell a little. Why was I expecting the man to say he was paying? Why was I feeling some type of way because he wasn't?

After I got off the call with the professor, I had to look up the hotel. It was a luxurious five-star. I guess it did make sense for the board to pay. After all, Ross and Stone was an elite private college. They wouldn't send their students to any kind of hotel. We had the best campus experience. I quickly erased the thought of Professor Davenport having anything to do with paying for my flight, hotel, and meals.

When I ran the opportunity by my parents, they had questions, but they weren't too bad. Ariel had been on an internship. Even though mine wasn't an internship, they trusted the administration and instructors at Ross and Stone.

My mama helped me book my flight. Daddy looked into the hotel. They both were present when I called Professor Davenport back with my flight details. Once he booked the flight, he emailed the confirmation. Everything was set. I was on my way to Atlanta for a week with an experienced paid director who was doing well in the industry.

THE RECIPE OF A GODLY WOMAN IX: HOPE

My flight wasn't long at all. I had one layover. Not bad. Professor Davenport had given me instructions. Once my flight landed, I was supposed to meet a man to drive me to the hotel. After I got my bags, I called my mama to check in and followed the instructions Professor Davenport gave me. I ended up outside of the airport, standing in front of a black Mercedes-Benz. The man dressed in a black suit called my name,

"Miss Reynolds?"

"Yes," I smiled.

He reached out for my bags. He took my rolling suitcase and put it in the trunk while I got into the car. When he pulled up to the hotel, I realized how pretty the historic building was. The man came and opened the door for me. I got out as he opened the trunk to get my bag.

"Thank you," I said as he handed me luggage.

I pulled my suitcase inside the hotel. I stopped at the front desk to check-in.

"Hello, I'm here to check-in. DaNia Reynolds."

The lady began to peck at a keyboard.

"Okay, yes. Jett Davenport and DaNia Reynolds.

What? I thought I heard her wrong.

"Um, no. Just DaNia."

Oh yes. Sorry. I meant your name, DaNia. The room was paid for by Jett Davenport."

I eyed her. I was curious about the payment method.

"The payment was made with his card or mine?"

"It looks to be his card," she said, looking at the screen.

Just like I thought! That man paid for my room! He told me the department's board was paying for it! I couldn't allow myself to feel good about this man paying for my room. Before my heart allowed my mind to get to wondering about his attraction toward me, I shoved the feeling and thought away. He wasn't attracted to me!

The woman handed me the key card to my room.

"Thank you," I said, taking the card. I was trying to ignore the fact that I was still wondering why he paid for my room.

THE RECIPE OF A GODLY WOMAN IX: HOPE

DaNia

I had never been inside the Fox Theatre in Atlanta. When I walked into the auditorium, the entire space was grand and royal. I smiled, looking up at the beautiful blue ceiling. I had to go up the balcony before the week was over. I knew that view was going to be nice.

A man was headed my way. He was a young black man with a brown complexion and a low haircut. As he got closer, I realized who he was.

"DaNia Reynolds," he said, extending his hand.

"Hi," I smiled, shaking his hand. "You're Drew Phillips."

"I am," he smiled. "Nice to meet you."

"Nice to meet you as well," I said.

Drew began to walk back toward the stage. I followed him.

"How was your flight?"

"It was fine," I smiled.

"Have you ever been to Atlanta?"

"I haven't," I said.

"How do you like it?"

"It's different," I smiled.

"Yeah, I've heard."

"What does that mean?"

"You're from Crestview, right?"

"I am," I said.

"Small town versus big city."

"Well, yeah," I said. "Are you from here?"

"Yes, born and raised. Being at Ross and Stone in a small town was a culture shock, but don't worry. I'll be helping you out this week."

"Thanks," I said.

Drew took me backstage. I met the cast of his play. The production crew was working on staging items and scenes. Everyone seemed to be nice. I was looking forward to the rest of the week.

On the opening night, I tagged along with Drew. I could tell he was really passionate about his work. He wasn't just directing. He was doing things to make sure the play would be a success. He was helping cast members change for scenes. He didn't mind lifting or moving things with his crew. Once a scene ended, he was right in the wings, congratulating actors and actresses as they came off the stage. He was great to watch in action.

The second night was packed. There were more people there than at the opening night. The cast had loosened up. They were having more fun. I could tell they had been working hard before the performance. They didn't lose a moment of momentum.

On day three, rehearsal ended early. Drew wanted the cast and crew to rest up for the upcoming performance. He said they did a good job the first two nights and deserved the rest. I agreed with him. They were very outstanding.

I was on my way out of the auditorium when he stopped me.

"Hey, DaNia."

I stopped, turning around to him.

"Hey, Drew. What's up?"

"I'm just checking on you. Is everything okay? Everybody been treating you good?"

I smiled at how nice he was being. "Thanks. Yes, everyone is nice. I'm good."

"Aight," he smiled. "That's good to know. I don't want Davenport on my top about *his woman*."

Did he call me Professor Davenport's woman? I knew what I heard. I was completely caught off guard. I smiled. My smile had to stay there for a good minute. I was trying to get my heart to stop beating so fast.

"Yeah, thanks again," I said.

I caught a Lyft back to the hotel. As soon as it stopped, I got out, took out my phone, and called Professor Davenport. He answered on the first ring.

"Hey DaNia."

"Don't hey DaNia me," I said. I had figured him out. He was in Atlanta!

"What?" he asked me.

"You're in Atlanta!"

"Huh?" he asked me. I could tell he was laughing.

"Nothing is funny," I laughed. "Bring yo behind to my room! Now!"

"Yes, ma'am!" he said.

I took the elevator up to my room. I stood outside of my room, leaning against the door. It wasn't long before I saw Professor Davenport coming down the hallway in a pair of black basketball shorts and a light blue t-shirt.

"You standing outside the door," he laughed.

I tried my best not to laugh. I shook my head at him.

"Didn't I tell you not to laugh a few minutes ago?"

He stopped in front of me, laughing.

"You wanted me to come to your room. Let's go in the room."

I rolled my eyes at him, pushing the door open. We both walked in. The door closed behind me.

"You told Drew I was your woman!"

Professor Davenport slid his hands into the pockets of his shorts. Our eyes connected. He started to walk toward me. Before his body got close to mine, I stopped him with my right arm. My hand felt all of his abs.

"You told...that man...that I... was...your woman," I repeated.

The professor was still silent. Our eyes were still locked. He lowered his head. His lips were near my forehead. I could feel his warm breath. I closed my eyes as his body eased my hand back, causing my body to rest against the door. His lips were near my nose because I could smell his minty breath. My arm slowly eased down. His top lip gently grazed mine. My body tingled. My heart lifted my head while my mind said no. His bottom lip grazed mine. His hand was around my waist, our bodies were like magnets, and our lips were the seal. The man had kissed me for the first time, and I could not contain it. The more he kissed me, the more I indulged. I wrapped my arms around his neck. He began to move back toward my bed. He lifted his head, ending the moment. I took my arms from around his neck. He walked over to a chair in the room and sat down. I slowly walked over to my bed and eased down.

LATOYA GETER

Professor Jett Davenport

I pulled back from her because we needed to talk. Yes, I had been wanting to kiss her for a long time, but I didn't want things to go like that. I was just so attracted to her. I had some things we needed to discuss before we even tried something. I started by explaining my actions. I didn't want her to get the wrong impression of me.

"My apologies for kissing you like that. I've just been wanting to for so long."

DaNia then said, "I kissed you back. You weren't by yourself."

We both were quiet. I didn't know why she was quiet. I knew I was trying to get myself to calm down. I was hoping she didn't see my guy poking.

"We need to talk," I said.

"I agree. I hope we have time. I have to be back at the theatre by four. It's noon."

"Okay. You wanna get something to eat and talk, or talk here?"

"We don't need any interruptions. I would rather stay here. I need to hear everything from you."

"I'm not tryna hold back anything from you."

"But you have," she said.

I wasn't letting her off the hook.

"And you haven't?"

THE RECIPE OF A GODLY WOMAN IX: HOPE

"Looks like we both have been holding things back from each other. The kiss revealed that."

She was right. I ran my hand down my face, thinking about how long I had held my feelings back from her.

"To pick up where we left off," I said. "I did tell Drew you were my woman. I knew he would be interested in you. He is a younger man. I didn't want him to pursue the woman I want."

I went ahead and told her the truth. Her kiss told me she was attracted to me. There was no need to keep holding things back.

"How did you find out?" I asked her. "Did he try to hit on you? What did he say?"

"No," said DaNia. "He mentioned he had to make sure I was okay. He didn't want you mad at him for not taking care of his woman."

"Alright," I said. "I didn't think he would still try to hit on you after I told him you were mine."

"How did I even come up?"

"He asked me about you when you first got here that night. He said you were attractive. He asked what did I know about you."

"That's when you told him I was your woman?"

"I didn't tell him that…"

"Okay! What did you tell him?"

"I told him me, and you have been dating for a year—"

She cut me off mid-sentence.

"Improv! Beginner Improvisation! That was my first class where I had you as my instructor!"

"That was the first time our eyes met."

She smiled, looking away from me.

"I remember."

"I've been wanting you since."

DaNia started to speak. "Professor I—"

"Jett," I said. "Please call me Jett."

I didn't know why I told her to call me by my first name. I wasn't ready to hear her say my name.

"Jett, you haven't been alone."

There it was. She said my name softly, which had my guy rising again. I had just calmed big fella down. When she told me I wasn't alone, I knew what I had expected over the years was true.

She continued to explain her feelings. "I didn't think you were attracted to me. Well, I wasn't sure. Even if I had known the truth, I probably wouldn't have known what to say. You're my professor."

"I understand that," I said to her. "I didn't say anything because you were my student at the time. I didn't want to complicate things."

DaNia said, "You don't teach senior-level classes, huh?"

"I don't," I said with a smile.

DaNia smiled at me before rolling her eyes with a light laugh.

"I won't have you my senior year. So you waited?"

"I did. The time is right."

DaNia lowered her head. She closed her eyes. She moved her neck from left to right. She slowly lifted her head with her eyes still closed.

"Professor, I mean, Jett, timing may seem right to you, but my life right now does not say a relationship. I'm gonna be honest with you. When I was late to

THE RECIPE OF A GODLY WOMAN IX: HOPE

your class, not performing well, falling asleep, and being out with an unexcused absence, I was in a relationship. We're not together now. I'm saying all this to say I just got out of a relationship. I don't need to jump into another one."

I appreciated her honesty. I needed to know exactly what I was walking into. No matter what she told me, I wasn't going to let it stop me from pursuing her. I just needed to know how to handle situations if they did come up.

"I'm not tryna rush you," I said to her. "I'm willing to take my time. I want to take my time with you. I do have one question. What will I be walking into? Whatever it is, I won't let it stop me from having you later. I need to know to ensure I don't add to what you're dealing with. I want to help ease your mind. I'm not trying to add stress."

DaNia stared at me for a second. She then said,

"Professor, don't play with me."

"Play with you..." I repeated.

"Don't even try to play with me, Jett."

What was going on? What was she talking about? I was confused! Why would I play with her feelings?

"DaNia, I'm not playing with you. Didn't we establish that already?"

"We have a lot more to talk about," she said. "You want me to tell you about my last relationship, and we haven't even talked about the one obvious thing between us. I'm young, but I'm not naïve. You're not about to play with me."

I didn't know what she was trying to say. I wanted her just to say what was on her mind. I tried to think about what she could have been talking about. Nothing was coming to my mind.

"DaNia, I don't know what could have you thinking I'm playing with you."

She sighed and said, "Our ages."

"Our ages," I repeated.

"Yes! I'm twenty-two–"

"And I'm thirty-four," I said. "What does that have to do with anything? I'm grown. You're grown."

"My age doesn't bother you?"

I let out a sigh. Yeah, I thought about our age difference, but that wasn't what I was worried about! I was more concerned about her education. My concern had nothing to do with her being my student. I didn't want to distract her from finishing school. I also couldn't let her slip away. I definitely couldn't allow a young man such as Drew to shoot his shot and take my woman.

"No, DaNia. Your age doesn't bother me. Now that you know how old I am, will my age be an issue?"

"I like my man to be older than me," she said. "I've just never been with one much older than me."

"It will be new for both of us," I said.

DaNia squinted at me. "Are you saying I'm the first young woman you've dated?"

I bit my bottom lip and smiled. "Oh, so we are going to try this thang out?"

DaNia shook her head and laughed. "Are you saying if I decide to date you, I will be the first young woman you've dated?"

"Don't change it up," I laughed. "But to answer your question, yes."

I got up from the chair and walked over to the bed, sitting next to her.

"I don't know what you're thinking. I can tell you over and over that I'm not trying to take advantage of you because you're young. It's still going to be up to you to believe me. I'm fine with that because I plan to show you anyway."

DaNia's eyes found mine. I stared back into them. There were two slow blinks from her before she looked away. I turned her head back to me.

"What happened in your last relationship that is going to have me working to prove just how much I want you?"

DaNia moved her head from fingers. "I'm not telling you until you tell me about your last relationship. Was she your wife or what?"

I didn't mind telling DaNia about my previous relationships with women. I went right into it.

"I've never been married. I don't have children. I thought I would get that one out of the way. Going back to the age thing, me and her are the same age. She wasn't woman enough to tell me she was married."

"Oh wow," said DaNia.

"Yep. I found out when her husband answered her phone one night while she was sleeping."

"That's crazy," said DaNia.

"Age doesn't always determine maturity," I said.

DaNia slowly looked up at me. My eyes found her eyes. Before I got stuck again, I said,

"Your turn."

DaNia took a deep breath and let it out. "There is another guy who wants to be with me. I won't tell him why I walked away from my ex. I don't want to put my ex-boyfriend's business out. Besides, the guy will use it to his advantage. I don't need that from anybody. Not from him or from you."

"What did I say a few minutes ago?"

"I heard you.." she said. "I need you to hear me."

"I'm listening. You started about being honest. I think you are mature enough to answer this. You still have feelings for your ex, huh?"

"I do," she said. "But I can't help him. I have to move on with my life."

"Help him with what?"

"I'll just say he is mentally unstable."

"You don't have to say anymore. I don't know him, but I am an advocate for mental health. I believe in therapy."

"He's in a mental health facility."

"That may sound bad to you, but he's getting treatment."

DaNia got up from the bed. "I don't really want to keep talking about it. I do have to move forward. I have to take my time moving forward."

I got up from the bed. I walked over to her, taking her hand into mine.

"We don't have to keep talking about your previous relationship. We can also take as much time as we need to build ours properly. There is no rush. I know what I'm up against."

"Thank you for understanding," she said, turning around to face me.

THE RECIPE OF A GODLY WOMAN IX: HOPE

"All I can do is try to understand," I said.

I looked at my phone. She still had time before she went back to the theatre.

"You got some time before you go back. How about you relax, and I'mma order room service."

DaNia kicked off her shoes. She climbed into bed, sliding under the comforter. I was sitting on the edge of the bed, looking at the menu of the restaurant that was inside the hotel. I heard her call my name. I turned around to see what she needed.

"The theatre department's board did not pay for flight or hotel.."

I laughed. I was waiting on her to figure it all out.

"They didn't," I said. "You better get used to me doing things for you."

I smiled at her and handed her the menu. "Find you something to eat so I can order it."

DaNia took the menu from me. "You just make sure you don't fall off."

I laughed. "Woman, you don't know who you're dealing with. You'll soon find out."

# *DaNia*

The food from the hotel was so good. I had to take a nap afterward. I was going to be late going back to the theatre. Jett handled that for me by calling Drew. Apparently, it worked. When I arrived an hour after our report time, Drew was acting like I came on time.

The entire night I was there, I wasn't focused. I helped cast members get dressed, but I wasn't focused on them. I was thinking about Jett. I was helping backstage, making sure sets were ready to go, but I wasn't focused on that either. Jett was still on my mind. Even while checking on things with Drew, Jett was on my mind.

I was supposed to call him when I was ready to go. He had already been heavy on my mind. I couldn't call him. The constant thought of him was a little scary. Especially since we had just confessed, we were attracted to one another. I decided not to call him. I called a Lyft instead.

As the Lyft pulled up to the hotel, I felt my phone vibrating. I saw Jett was calling me. I stared at the phone for a quick second. I didn't answer it. I texted him instead.

"I made it to the hotel."

He immediately texted back.

"What happened to me coming to get you?"

THE RECIPE OF A GODLY WOMAN IX: HOPE

"I just needed some time to think."

"Okay," he said.

I didn't text him back. I headed up to my room and took a shower. After my shower, I climbed into bed. With the comforter covering me up, I tried to sleep, but once again, Jett was on my mind. I stared at the ceiling. I rolled over to look out of the window. I pulled the comforter back from my body. I couldn't sleep. I tossed and turned in the bed. I then heard my text tone. I picked my phone up from the nightstand. Jett had texted me.

"Are you sleeping?"

"I'm up," I replied. "I can't sleep."

Jett replied with three numbers. I didn't have to ask what the set of numbers was. I sat up in bed, thinking about my next decision. Man, it was too early! Both of us had wanted one another for a long time. Maybe it wasn't. We sort of knew one another. I knew the professor, but I didn't know the professor. I didn't take him to be the type to try to sleep with me so soon. Temptation was knocking at my door! I sure wasn't Ariel, but I for sure wasn't Arbrielle! At that moment, I didn't know who I was. I was still in love with a man struggling mentally, or maybe I had been dealing with him for so long that I felt guilty for walking away. Either way, I was not okay! I couldn't leave out Haze! I didn't want to settle, but he was persistent. He wasn't quite my type, but he wasn't bad-looking. I was hoping that he could change, but he wasn't who I wanted. I wanted Jett.

The number 318 stared back at me. My eyes closed. My nose took in air while my body released it. My hand lifted, knocking on the hotel room door. The door slowly opened. Behind it was Jett. Where was his shirt? Why was this man standing in front of me with the sexiest built body I had ever seen? His chiseled chest begged for me to run my index finger down it.

"You coming in?" he asked me in the softest, deepest voice.

I was stuck! I couldn't move. I didn't know what to do. Lord knows I wasn't trying to sleep with this man, but I was already standing in front of the hotel room. I slowly looked up into his eyes.

"Professor I —"

"Jett," he said.

I started over again. "Jett, I don't know why I'm standing right here. What I do know is I've thought about you all night. I couldn't focus on the play. I couldn't sleep. I'm also trying to process that the guy who I thought was for me is not. Another guy could change. Then there's you. My college professor, who I've wanted for years but was too afraid to cross that student-professor boundary. Timing is so terrible!"

I let it all out! I had to! My feelings were all over the place! He said he would try to understand me. I was *hoping* he would keep his word.

"Come in, DaNia," he said.

I shook my head no. "I can't sleep with you."

"Sleep with me..." he repeated.

"I can't do it," I said.

Jett eyed me. He took a step back. "I'm not sleeping with you. I'm not trying to sleep with you. I won't ever just sleep with you. Your vulnerability won't allow me to do that. I'm not referring to taking advantage of that vulnerability. Your honesty and

THE RECIPE OF A GODLY WOMAN IX: HOPE

ability to be vulnerable is not only the biggest turn-on, but it's making me want to protect you and provide you with the security you deserve. I need to cater to you emotionally, mentally, spiritually, and yes, physically."

My heart was already easing. He took my hands into his. "I'm trying to start things off right so that when it is time for me to make love to you, you'll feel protected and secure."

He began to lead me into the room. My legs followed. I heard the room door close. My heart told me he wasn't lying. My thoughts were telling me otherwise.

Jett sat on the edge of the bottom of the king-size bed. His thumbs rubbed the top of my hands. His voice filled my ears.

"You said you couldn't sleep. If you have something on your mind, I'll listen. "

I stared into his eyes. They told me I could say what was on my mind.

"I do have some things on my mind. I mean, we've talked about them already, and I don't want you to feel like I don't believe you, but —"

"You need assurance," he said, finishing my statement. "There is nothing wrong with that. For our future, tell me what you need, and I'll make sure it's handled. I don't need a long, drawn-out explanation to defend your needs."

"I do need to be sure that all of this is not in my head. I need to know I'm making this up. I have so much going on."

Jett slid up the bed. He rested his back on the set of pillows. He pulled back the covers. He reached out his arms for me. I stepped out of my crocs before climbing into the bed. I crawled up to him. He held the covers back for me. I snuggled under, and he pulled me close. His body was so warm. He felt so good. I felt his hand caressing my waist.

"You can ask me all the questions you need to clear your mind so that you can sleep."

I looked up at him. His eyes met mine. I started the questions with,

"How is this gonna work?"

THE RECIPE OF A GODLY WOMAN IX: HOPE

Professor Jett Davenport

I needed her to be more specific. Maybe she didn't know how to ask me what was on her mind. I had a feeling I knew what she was trying to ask me. I took a shot at it.

"We've already been through the age. You're no longer my student. We took care of that, but I will assure you that those two things won't be a problem."

DaNia then said, "Okay, but I'm still in school. I live with my parents. You're in your career. You have a family business, probably a whole house. How am I supposed to fit into your life?"

I leaned my head back on the pillows, taking in her question. I actually had thought about how I would fit into her life.

"I'm not trying to stand in your way. I want you to finish school. I want you to be a successful actress or director. One day you'll leave your parents. We all have lived with our parents. Maybe one day your father will bless me to have you forever. I am in my career. I can go to work and spend time with you when you're available. I'm not going to stop you from living your life. If I could experience it with you, I would be the fortunate one. About my house, I'm *hoping* that you'll visit one day."

DaNia smiled at me. When her smile faded, her eyes told me she had more on her mind. I rubbed my finger down her cheek.

"What else?"

"I already have a daddy. Daniel is enough. I'm named after the man. I don't need another one."

I laughed. I knew she was going back to my age. Our outlooks on our age difference were very different.

"DaNia, I'm not trying to be your daddy. I'm trying to be your partner, your man. I'm not even old enough to be your dad. I was twelve when you were born. I'm definitely old enough to be your brother."

"People will talk," she said to me. "Especially the folks in Crestview. I'm shocked my parents didn't hear about me eating in the café with you. My mama had it rough growing up there. Things were bad when she and my daddy started dating. They had a big issue when they got married. Mama held it together so people didn't get a chance to talk. They made it through their issues. Our family may not be the hot topic, but the folks are watching us hard, waiting for one of the children to slip up. My big brother held on. Ariel did, too. Arbrielle put the light back on our family, but she has got her life on track. Crestview is waiting to see which twin is going to slip up. Me or my brother."

Who didn't know about the Reynolds family? Everyone in Crestview and surrounding cities knew about the work Daniel did and was continuing to do in Crestview.

"Your father has inspired me for years," I said to her. "I didn't know I would find his daughter attractive. I was at Ross and Stone when Arbrielle attended. I was an adjunct. I heard about her, but when you became my student, I saw something different than what I had heard about your sister. Everyone in the art department knew about Ariel. I felt you had your own mark to make. I still feel that way."

DaNia smiled, looking up at me. I smiled back at her and said,

"So you know I wouldn't do anything to jeopardize your family's reputation or jeopardize you having the opportunity to make your mark. *I'm not trying to put you in difficult situations or leave you to face anything alone.* If the people in Crestview talk, let me handle it. I have Ross and Stone handled, too."

"I'm not weak by a long shot," she said. "I can handle anything. My mama ain't raise no punks! I'm just saying I don't have time to deal with them."

I laughed again. I liked that her sense of humor was starting to show.

"I'm not attracted to weak women," I said to her. "But as your man, you're going to have to let me handle things for you."

"So, add you to my show-out list?"

"Show out list," I laughed.

DaNia looked at me and said, "When it doubt, call my daddy, brothers, and uncles. They all will show out!"

I laughed some more. "Yeah, add me to the list. Right after your uncles so I can work my way to the top."

DaNia smiled at me. She moved in closer to me before saying,

"I want to be a mother. How do you feel about kids?"

I gently lifted her leg, placing it around mine. I was now facing her with our bodies connected.

"I want a family," I smiled. "I want children. I don't care how many. I've dated women. I took risks with some, but they weren't right for me."

DaNia yawned. She closed her eyes and opened them again.

"I've only been with one other guy..."

She closed her eyes again. She was close to falling asleep. I saw her open her eyes once more.

"We never had sex."

Da'Nia closed her eyes. They stayed closed for a minute. She opened them again.

"I just want to be stable when I get ready to have a baby."

Da'Nia looked up at me. Her eyes closed again. She opened them again. She sat up in the bed. I realized she was fighting her sleep. I wanted to know why.

"Why won't you just go to sleep?"

With her back to me, she said,

"I wanna believe that you aren't trying to sleep with me."

I sat up, rubbing her back. "DaNia, I'm not trying to sleep with you. You're fragile right now. You're a

THE RECIPE OF A GODLY WOMAN IX: HOPE

virgin. That doesn't surprise me. I have to take my time with you. I've been waiting for you, now I have to be patient. I will be. I believe you're worth it. Lay back down. I'm just trying to hold you."

DaNia turned and looked at me. Our eyes connected like they always did. I laid back down in the bed. DaNia eased back down into my arms. I pulled her close to me. She snuggled up into my body. I leaned my head back on the pillows behind me before closing my eyes.

LATOYA GETER

DaNia

A bold, masculine, but sweet fragrance filled my nose. My eyes opened to see white sheets. I didn't see Jett in the bed. I rolled over to see my phone on the nightstand. I picked it up. It was ten in the morning. Which meant it was nine at home. I had a missed Facetime call from my sisters. I Facetimed them back. Arbrielle joined the call first.

"Hey Nianee!"

She had been calling me that since I could remember. No matter how old I got, she was still going to call me that.

"Hey, Bri," I said.

Ariel joined the call.

"Hey, y'all! Good morning!"

"Morning, big sis!" I said.

"Hey, sister big!" laughed Arbrielle. "Where is my baby?"

Our niece, baby Audrey, was a busy toddler.

"Her daddy is giving her a bath. I'm cooking breakfast."

"Nianee, how is it going with the play?" asked Arbrielle. "You like Atlanta?"

"The director is cool. The cast is fun to be around. They are doing good with their nights and attendance. Atlanta is nothing like Crestview, but it's not bad."

"I'm glad you're enjoying the experience," said Ariel.

"I knew you wouldn't be too fond of the big city," said Arbrielle.

Ariel agreed with her. "Right! That's yo thang, Bri. She loves the small city life."

"Give me Vegas! Houston! LA! I'mma turn up!" said Bri.

I laid back down in the bed, listening to my sister. I heard the hotel door open.

"DaNia, I brought you breakfast, sweetheart."

My sisters immediately stopped talking. They heard him! I couldn't even turn and look at Jett! I didn't take my attention off the screen.

"That's a dude's voice," said Ariel.

"Dude!" said Arbrielle. "That voice was deep as hell! That's a grown man!"

"Who is that, DaNia?" asked Ariel. "You got a man in there?"

"You went to Atlanta for a man instead of school," said Arbrielle. "I love it! Are you being rebellious like me?"

"He has breakfast for you!" said Ariel.

Jett whispered, "Who is that? My bad. I'm sorry. I didn't know you were on the phone."

My sisters heard him whispering.

"Don't whisper now!" laughed Ariel.

"Yeah!" laughed Arbrielle. "As a matter of fact, come to the phone. We need to see you!"

"Woah!" I laughed. "Hold on!"

I muted the phone, looking at Jett.

"Don't mute us trick!" said Arbrielle.

I laughed so hard.

"My sisters are on the phone."

"I'll say hello," he said.

My eyes widened. He was actually willing to show his face. Jett then said,

"I plan to meet them one day anyway."

I was so afraid for them to meet him. Especially Arbrielle. She knew him. I unmuted the phone.

"First of all," I said. "He and I are taking things slow. I didn't come to Atlanta for a man. I came for school. We knew we were attracted to one another. We didn't know how the other person felt. We have an understanding now."

"Okay!" said Arbrielle. "Where is he?"

"Bri, she may want to wait," said Ariel.

"What? Wait? Girl! People meet folks, and they end up married and divorced!" said Arbrielle.

"She has a point," said Jett.

Arbrielle ate that up! "Look, even he agrees. Let us see the man!"

Jett smiled. I shook my head at him. Before I gave him the phone, I said to Arbrielle,

"Control yourself."

"I'm yo big sister!" she laughed.

"I'm saying that because you know him."

"I know him!" she repeated. "Hurry up and let us see him!"

I handed Jett the phone.

"Professor Davenport!" screamed Arbrielle.

Ariel laughed. "Oh wow! I've heard about your work at Ross and Stone. You weren't there when I was there."

THE RECIPE OF A GODLY WOMAN IX: HOPE

"Hey, ladies," he smiled. "Nice to see you, Arbrielle. It's good to finally meet the best artist of her time, Ariel Reynolds."

"Hey, Professor!" laughed Arbrielle.

"Nice to meet you as well," said Ariel.

"DaNia!" said Arbrielle.

"Yes," I laughed, sliding into the camera.

"I'm proud of you! Great catch! All the females at Ross and Stone be drooling over Mr. Jett Davenport! So when they find out, call me, and you know I'm on the way."

"You won't have to worry about that," said Jett. "We won't go public until after she graduates. Plus, like she said, we're going to take our time."

"I like to hear that," said Ariel. "My sister has worked hard. We don't need any distractions. She's a Reynolds."

"I am aware of the family legacy," said Jett. Your father is a man I admire. I'm not ruining anything for DaNia."

"Great," smiled Ariel. "Speaking of daddy. DaNia, when are you going to break the news."

Jett then said, "You already know where I stand. I'm going to hop in the shower. I'll let you and your sisters handle that. Take care, ladies."

"You as well," smiled Ariel.

"Since you are with my sister, I can call you Jett now. Bye Jett!" said Arbrielle.

"See ya later, Arbrielle," laughed Jett.

I then answered Ariel. "Of course, I'm not telling Daddy today or when I get back. I'mma talk to Mama."

"Talk to Mama," said Ariel.

Once I heard the hotel bathroom door close, the shower came on. I then said to my sisters.

"Yes, talk to Mama. He paid for everything! Not Ross and Stone."

"Oh, he did," smiled Arbrielle.

"Yes!"

"What's the issue?" asked Ariel. "The real issue! Cause Mama and Daddy ain't mad at a man doing things for us."

"He's 34!" I said.

Arbrielle shrugged her shoulders. "He looks 24! Fine as hell!"

"Bri!" I snapped.

Arbrielle laughed. "You mad 'cause yo man fine?"

Ariel interjected. "Bri, stop," she laughed. "On a serious note, he is not much older than you. It ain't like the man twice yo age! It's okay."

"He's twelve years older than me."

Ariel reminded me of the age difference between our parents.

"Mama and Daddy are ten years apart.

She was right, and I hadn't thought about their age difference. I instantly started to feel better.

THE RECIPE OF A GODLY WOMAN IX: HOPE

Professor Jett Davenport

I came out of the bathroom from my shower. DaNia was staring at her phone in the middle of the bed. I noticed she wasn't in the middle of a call. She looked up at me. Our eyes didn't connect like they normally would. Something was wrong. With a towel around my waist, I sat on the side of the bed.

"I can tell something is up."

DaNia didn't hold it back from me.

"Drew called. He's on his way to the emergency room. His assistant director is with him. He's not feeling well. He's leaving me in charge this evening."

"I hate to hear that about Drew. That is good for you. Congratulations. Why do you seem down about it?"

"I'm nervous!"

"It's normal and natural to be nervous. You got this. Drew wouldn't have left you in charge if he didn't feel you couldn't lead the cast and crew. This is a great opportunity."

"Thanks," she said.

"You're welcome. You know, I feel like you got it. You are more than capable of directing this evening."

My cell then started to ring. I picked it up from the hotel table. Drew was calling me.

"What's up, Drew?" I answered, placing the phone on speaker.

"Davenport. I'm on my way to the ER. Mane, it may be food poisoning. I don't know, but I'm sick. I'm not going to be able to make it tonight. My assistant is with me. I called DaNia already, but I wanted to call you. She's in charge tonight. She has it, but I know you'll be there to support her. She sounded a little nervous."

"You know I got you. I'll make sure she's good before we go. Yeah, she can handle it. She's one of the best. You take care of yourself. Keep me updated."

"Aight, Davenport. Thanks again. Tell DaNia thank you and that I said she's gonna be good."

"I'll let her know," I said, ending the call with Drew. I looked over at DaNia and smiled. "See, we both know you got this! You have to know you got it."

DaNia looked up at me and smiled. "I'mma do my best."

I walked over to the edge of the bed where she was. Running my finger gently down her face, I smiled.

"You're gonna do a superb job. I'mma be right there with you."

DaNia wasn't confident that she could lead the group. They normally met early before the show. I made the executive decision for the cast and crew to come in three hours before the show instead of five. DaNia was nervous. She needed to calm her nerves. I knew exactly what she needed.

She thought she was going back to her room. I didn't let that happen. She stayed in my room. I told

THE RECIPE OF A GODLY WOMAN IX: HOPE

her to relax while I made a couple of trips to pick up some things. I didn't tell her where I was going or what I was going to pick up. I tried not to stay gone too long. I had time to help ease her mind, but I didn't have a lot of time.

When I came back to the room, she was still there. She saw the plastic bags I was carrying. She got to asking me questions. I laughed because she was being nosey. I slid into the bathroom and locked the door behind me. I didn't want her to see what I was doing for her.

LATOYA GETER

DaNia

I unbuckled my seatbelt. People started to stand up to depart the plane. I hated carry-on bags. I only carried my purse as I eased out of my seat in first class.

My parents picked me up from the airport. They were already waiting for me at baggage claim. I hugged them both. Daddy kissed me on my cheek. Mama squeezed me tight.

"Thank God you made it home safely," said Daddy.

"Yes," said Mama. "That layover had me worried. I was so happy you saved some money. It came in handy for that long-delayed flight."

My connecting flight was delayed. I did check in with my parents. I did have money left over from my trip, but I didn't spend it. I didn't tell my parents that Jett was on the flight with me. He made sure I had everything I needed.

When my daddy went to get my bags, I hurried and turned to my mama.

"I need to talk to you."

"What's up, baby girl?"

"Not here. Not with Daddy."

Mama eyed me. She looked concerned.

"It's nothing bad. I need your opinion about someone."

THE RECIPE OF A GODLY WOMAN IX: HOPE

"Someone..."

"Yes."

"You don't want to talk here or around your daddy. Is it about Lil Greg?"

"No."

Mama squinted at me.

"The Haze guy?"

"No," I said again.

Daddy coming back over with my luggage stopped us from talking. Mama smiled at him.

"You have the bags, honey."

"Yep," he smiled. "Let's get our baby girl home so she can rest."

Daddy drove us home. Mama rode in the passenger seat while I sat in the back of her red Chevrolet Blazer. He pulled into our driveway.

"Alright, baby girl. You head on in. I got your bag."

"Thank you, Daddy."

I opened the back door and got out of the car. Mama got out of the passenger's side. We both met in front of the SUV. We began to walk up the driveway.

"Mama, I can't talk here. Can we go somewhere?"

"Um, no. We just got you home. Your daddy is going to be asking questions."

"Mama, I can't talk with him around."

"Well, you're gonna have to. If we leave, he is going to be asking questions."

"Mama, I really need to talk to you."

"Okay. I did hear him mention something about leaving to go out with your uncles. We can talk if he leaves. If he doesn't leave, can it wait until tonight?"

"Yes, ma'am," I said.

I went with Mama's plan. She was right. I didn't want Daddy asking questions. Mama didn't believe in keeping things from him. I wasn't going to make things hard for her.

Right after Daddy brought my luggage to my room, while sitting on my bed, I heard a light knock on my door. Mama peeped her head in. She came in, closing the door behind her.

"Your daddy did go ahead and leave to meet your uncles. We have some time to ourselves. Now, when I asked you if you needed to talk about Lil Greg, you said no. I asked you about the Haze guy, and you said no. So is there someone else?"

"Yes, ma'am," I said.

Mama slowly nodded her head.

"You met someone in Atlanta?"

"I didn't meet him in Atlanta. We already knew one another. We both have been attracted to one another. We've never said anything. We knew, but certain circumstances prevented us from expressing our feelings. He was in Atlanta. We used that time to put everything on the table."

Mama knew me like a book. She didn't respond, she just said,

"You want to tell me more, go ahead."

I crossed my legs, fidgeting with my fingers.

"I'm gonna just get the bad parts out of the way."

Mama laughed. "Do you know how many talks I've had like this before? You and your sisters act like I wasn't young. Ariel ran to Kim, but I knew. We eventually talked. Arbrielle, well, everyone knew I

THE RECIPE OF A GODLY WOMAN IX: HOPE

was going to break her neck, but the conversations got better over the years. Now I'm having it with you for the first time. You and Lil Greg just synced together, so I get it, but because we are having a new conversation that's not about the Haze boy, and you wanna discuss bad things, I feel like this is going to be your official talk with me. So I've done it all, and your sisters have prepared me for my baby. Plus, you're so much like me. I'm ready. Give me what you got."

"Since you said I'm just like you, I'll start there. Ariel already helped me a little.

"You've talked to your big sisters. That's good."

"Well, I was on a Facetime call with them when he came in the room."

"Really?" laughed Mama. "So they met him?"

"Just on Facetime," I laughed.

"I'm so hurt," she joked, grabbing her heart. "We talk every day, and you hid him in the background. Must have told him to be quiet 'cause your mama was calling."

"I didn't exactly say that," I laughed.

Mama smiled at me. "You're laughing. Whatever you need to tell me must not be too bad."

I went right into our age difference.

"Mama, he's twelve years older than me."

Mama nodded her head, looking out into space. She smiled, tilting her head to the right. She closed her eyes, and her smile grew bigger. She opened her eyes, still staring into space.

"I was in the library working on my homework when your daddy came in. We got to messing with one another. He told me he was a professor. I called him old." She laughed, remembering the moment. "I tried to guess his age. I guessed wrong on purpose. I told him he was a 54-year-old geezer."

I laughed while my mama shared the moment with me.

"He called me a young buck. I had to buck back! I learned he was ten years older than me that day. I was twenty-four."

My heart stopped for a second. I heard Mama, but I needed to say it for myself.

"Daddy was thirty-four."

Mama slowly turned her head, smiling at me.

"The same age as the man you're dating."

"Dating," I repeated. "How did you know? I mean, we've agreed to take things slow until I graduate."

"You're talking to me about him. Something is going on. I raised you and your sisters with intention. I never wanted to be disconnected from you all. God blessed me to have three girls to have relationships that I didn't have with my mother. I know when a man has hurt my babies. When one has upset you all and when one is bringing happiness into your lives."

Mama was making our conversation so easy. I didn't have an issue with telling her,

"He is a professor at Ross and Stone. He was one of my professors. He's not teaching me this fall or spring."

Mama smiled. "Younger versions of me and your father."

"I realized that, too!" I smiled.

Mama then said, "Both of you decided to wait before you get into a full relationship?"

THE RECIPE OF A GODLY WOMAN IX: HOPE

"Yes, ma'am," I said. "I didn't hold back from him. I told him I wasn't having any distractions. He understood. He wants me to finish school."

"Sounds good," said Mama. "Is this the professor who came to the play?"

"Yes!" I smiled. "So, see, you did meet him."

"Chile, I wasn't paying too much attention to him. I thought Haze would be the one."

I laughed. "Mama, I told you I wasn't too much worried about him."

"I see! You had the professor on ya mind."

"He had me on his mind, too!"

"I heard that," laughed Mama.

"He also paid for the trip. I wanted to let you know."

"Well, that's not a bad thing. He spoke with me and your father. You got there safe. You made it back. I don't see any problem. His actions tell me that he is already invested in your success."

"We talked about my future and how we would fit into one another's lives.

"How do you feel about that?"

"We will be able to work it out."

Mama smiled. "All you can do is give it a try."

I was fine with trying out the whole dating thing with Jett. I had to be honest with myself. I couldn't handle the gestures he was throwing my way. I needed to see how Mama handled Daddy while she was younger.

"Mama, how did you handle the things Daddy threw at you?"

Mama looked so confused.

"Your daddy didn't throw things at me. Are you asking how did I handle being with an older man? As in knowing what he wanted and being upfront about his feelings?"

"Yes! Plus the things he did for you."

Mama smiled. She was back staring into space.

"I tried to play hard to get at first. I didn't trust him. I didn't trust anybody. He never gave up on me. Once I realized he wasn't giving up, my response to him wasn't as bitter. I wasn't used to a man doing things for me. He was being genuine first without taking from me. Once we started to date, I still didn't think it was real. I struggled at first. I was so independent. I had to learn to step back and let him be my man."

"The things Jett did in Atlanta, I never experienced any of that with Lil Greg."

"Jett is older than Lil Greg. He has experience. Plus, he has obviously wanted to be with you for a long time. What happened in Atlanta? Did you sleep with him?"

I was always honest with my mama. I felt if I told her the truth, she would be able to give me the right advice. I never understood how lying to your parents led to getting the help you needed.

"I wanted to," I said. "That's why I asked how did you handle the things Daddy did for you. The first time he held me, we talked until I fell asleep. He listened to me and understood my situation with Lil Greg and Haze. I was a little uncomfortable at first. Once we established I wasn't in the right mindset for the next step, I felt better."

THE RECIPE OF A GODLY WOMAN IX: HOPE

I then thought about when Jett left the hotel and came back with bags full of items.

"Mama, the man ran me a bath. I was nervous about directing the play. I've seen bubble baths in movies."

Mama laughed so hard.

"No! Wait! I've seen bubble baths in movie scenes. I've never thought about a rose petal bath. The entire tub was filled with roses."

I had to tell mama everything from start to finish. I closed my eyes, thinking about the evening. It was one I would never forget. My heart told my mind they would cherish the moment forever.

I was sitting in the bed inside of the hotel room. I heard the door open. I could see bags.

"What are you doing? What do you have in those bags?"

Jett yelled from the bathroom, "You're supposed to be relaxing, not worrying about what I have going on."

I heard the bathroom door close. I started to flip through the channels on the TV. Nothing seemed to interest me. I cut the television off. I laid my head back on one of the pillows. I stared at the ceiling. I closed my eyes for a second. At least, I thought it was for a second until I felt Jett's hand on my face. He was gently rubbing my face. I had fallen asleep. He held his hand out for me. I sat up in the bed, taking his hand. He gently pulled me up from the bed, leading me to the bathroom. He eased the bathroom door open. Rose petals filled the tub. I knew there was water in the tub because the steam filled the room, but not a spec of water or bubbles could be seen. Only rose petals. There were two candles on the far edges of the tub. Jett sat on the edge of the tub. He pulled me toward him. He undressed me, starting with my shorts. He eased my t-shirt up. When he realized I did not have a bra on, he slowly pulled my shirt down. He stood up from the edge of the tub. With his eyes locked with mine, he leaned his head down toward mine. I closed my eyes, feeling a pinch of his breath on my lips before I heard his voice in my ear.

"I'll leave you to take off your shirt and panties. Enjoy your bath."

I fell back on the bed after telling my mama what happened in Atlanta.

"Mama! He wasn't trying to have sex with me at that moment. I knew that when he didn't take my shirt off. I appreciate him because its way too early. I'm trying to wait for marriage, but I was feeling things I've never felt before. I was finna give it to him."

Mama laughed. "Girl! Yo lil virgin behind wasn't about to give that grown man nothing! You aren't ready to meet him in that bedroom!"

"Leave me alone," I laughed.

Mama then said to me, "On a serious note, I do know how you feel. I remember the first time your daddy kissed me. He pulled back, and I went back for more. We had to set boundaries. We weren't having sex before marriage. Have you both set boundaries?"

"He doesn't want to have sex with me while I'm fragile. My vulnerability won't ever allow him to sleep with me."

THE RECIPE OF A GODLY WOMAN IX: HOPE

"Oh wow," said Mama. "You definitely aren't ready for him to make love to you."

"I immediately sat up in the bed, looking at Mama."

"He said that! How did you know?"

"He's a grown man!"

"Mama!"

"Don't Mama me. You must didn't set boundaries as it pertains to having sex with him."

I lowered my head. Mama lifted my chin.

"Your father and I told one another we would not get into your relationships. I've done good with your brother and sisters. I'm going to stay out of yours, too, *but I will say if you make decisions, be prepared for the consequences. They will come. You can't stop a consequence. You can only prevent them with your actions.*"

"Yes, ma'am," I said.

Mama gave me a hug. I hugged her back. I thanked her for always being there for me. She told me she would never leave me. She may not have always agreed with the things her children did, but she never stopped being a mother.

Mama got up from my bed. She walked to my bedroom door. Before opening the door, she turned back to me and said,

"I'll handle your daddy. Don't be in a rush to bring Jett home. Take your time."

"Yes, ma'am," I said, taking in why she told me to take my time.

LATOYA GETER

Professor Jett Davenport

Classes had started for the fall semester. I didn't have early morning classes. My first class started at ten. I still planned to be on campus early. I kept my same plan from the previous semester.

With my coffee and briefcase, I managed to open my office door. I walked into my office, sitting my coffee on my desk. I sat in my office chair. My phone started to ring. Drew was calling.

"Hey Drew, what's up," I said, answering my cell.

"Davenport, first day of classes, huh?"

"Yeah, I'm in my office now."

"I was calling about DaNia. My cast and crew are still talking about how good she did on the final night. Every transition was smooth. She was encouraging and was really positive. They had an overall good night with her. She graduates in the spring, right?"

"Yeah, she does."

"Let her know she has a job as a director. I'm writing a new play. I want it to go on tour, but I'm not stopping my current show. I'll have two shows on the road. She'll be directing the cast and crew of the new one."

"I'll definitely let her know. Thanks for letting me know. She's gonna like to hear what the cast and crew had to say."

"Aight, Davenport. Y'all let me know if she wants to direct, too."

"I got you," I said.

There was a knock on my door as I was ending the call with Drew.

"Come in," I said.

The door opened. My eyes met a pair of soft legs in sliver slide-in diamond shoes. My eyes traveled up to a light powder pink cotton loose dress. I leaned back in my office chair, locking eyes with DaNia. She closed my door behind her.

"Good morning," she said.

"I was having a good morning. Now I'm having a better morning."

I got up from the chair, and she walked over to me. Sliding my arm around her waist, I pulled her in for a hug.

"You smelling all good," I said as the strawberry mango scent filled my nose.

"Looking good. Legs out!"

DaNia laughed, running her fingers down my tie.

"Thank you. I've never seen this tie in class.

"It's new," I said. "You like it?"

"I do," she laughed.

I sat on the edge of my desk with her between my legs. She was resting her arms on my chest.

"Drew called," I said to her. "His cast and crew are still talking about the great job you did."

"Oh really," she said.

"Yep. There's more. Drew is writing a new show. He wants you to direct it once you graduate. Two shows on the road. One with you as the director."

DaNia's smile went away. She looked away for a second. She turned back to me.

"You know my dream is to act."

"I do know that."

"Are you supporting me or Drew? Which student?"

Her tone surprised me. I also couldn't believe she was really asking me that. I knew DaNia and I were going to have arguments and disagreements, but I was not ever going to argue with her about her goals and aspirations. Plus, I didn't mind answering her questions my way.

"Number one, you're not my student. Number two, I'm always going to support my woman. We're working on being together, so I'm ten thousand percent behind your acting career. I just wanted you to know what Drew had for you after graduation."

DaNia looked away from me. "Okay."

Her attitude took me back to the hotel room when she was nervous about directing the play.

"What's up with your tone and attitude?"

DaNia sighed. She turned her head back to me.

"It's the first last day of my college career. I'm graduating. I want to secure a role. I want to act. Not direct."

"You're worried about auditioning for roles?"

"Yes."

"Well, you shouldn't be. We got you in the department. When the casting directors come on campus, you do what you do. Everything will work out fine."

THE RECIPE OF A GODLY WOMAN IX: HOPE

DaNia leaned into my chest. She rested her head there. I wrapped my around her. We both were quiet for a minute. The silence helped ease the mood in the room.

"Friday evening. Can I take you out?" I asked her.

"Yeah," she said softly.

She eased up from my chest.

"What do I need to wear? You like surprises."

I laughed, thinking about how she wanted to know what was in the bags.

"I do plan on surprising you a lot."

DaNia smiled, shaking her head.

"Don't wear anything too fancy," I said.

She rolled her eyes. "That's not helping me."

I laughed and said, "Jeans and a T-shirt will be fine."

DaNia

Symone was sitting on her bed. I was sitting on the edge of my bed. We heard a knock on our dorm room door. I went to the door and opened it. Taylor walked in and sat at our desk.

"Now, why y'all all quiet?" she asked. "DaNia, you said you wanted to talk to us. You must have already told Symone."

"She ain't told me nothing," said Symone. "I'm quiet 'cause I'm waiting on her."

"It's not bad," I said.

"Well, why couldn't we go out or grab something to eat, and you tell us?"

"Y'all are too loud!"

"Too loud," emphasized Taylor.

"What does us being loud have to do with anything?"

"Because we, as in me and him, don't want our business out just yet."

"Him!" they both said a loud.

"Yes!" I laughed. "See how loud y'all were! That's why we couldn't go out and talk."

"Who is this guy?" asked Taylor.

"Or did you give Haze a chance?" asked Symone.

"Haze is not the guy," I said.

"You went back to Lil Greg?" asked Symone.

THE RECIPE OF A GODLY WOMAN IX: HOPE

"No…"

"A new guy!" said Symone. "Okaaay."

"He goes here?" asked Taylor.

"He was in Atlanta with me."

"In Atlanta!" they both said.

"We talked to you while you were there!" said Symone.

"You never said a word!" said Taylor.

"I needed to make sure I understood how we were going to handle things. We now have an understanding. We are working toward a relationship. We will definitely make things official after graduation."

"Oh, so y'all have been discussing some real things, huh?" asked Symone.

"We have," I said.

"Girl!" said Taylor. "I can't say that's good until I know who he is. He might not be the total package!"

I turned my head toward Taylor. I leaned back on my bed and said,

"Is Jett the full package?"

My girls screamed so loud!

"Professor Davenport!" said Symone.

"Stop playing!" said Taylor.

"I'm not playing!" I said.

"He is the total package!" said Taylor. "His fine ass!"

"He came to my play at home," I smiled. "I didn't tell y'all because I wasn't sure about his feelings. He paid for everything in Atlanta! He held me. I slept so good in his arms! We talked about everything. He made me a hot rose petal bath. It felt so good to ease down in the roses. We flew back together. He made sure I was okay during the flight delay."

"Yeeees! Rose petal bath!" said Symone.

"I knew he wanted you," said Taylor. "Girl! I'm so glad y'all are waiting after graduation to make things official. I would hate to have to slap one of these females in they mouth behind my girl!"

"Arbrielle said the same thing," I laughed.

"Sis, know how they are around here. You ain't dated no guy on campus. I have. They are some smart, wealthy hoes! They be coming from all different corners."

Me and Symone laughed at Taylor's description of the girls on campus.

"Glad my man is at home," said Symone.

"But don't worry about them," said Taylor. "I'm happy for you! If one of them do find out, we got yo back!"

"Yeah, you know we do," smiled Symone.

My friends came over to me, and we shared a group hug.

"We are so happy for you," said Symone.

"You deserve to be happy," said Taylor.

THE RECIPE OF A GODLY WOMAN IX: HOPE

Professor Jett Davenport

With the top down on the Audi S5 Convertible, DaNia sat on the passenger side, bobbing her head to Lauryn Hill's Can't Take My Eyes Off of You. I drove past the Addonsdale Welcome Sign. She cut the music down.

"Addonsdale! Please do not tell me you are about to have me around your family in jeans and a t-shirt."

"You're not meeting my family," I laughed. "Calm down. I would let you know that."

"We're in your home town! If we aren't going to be with your family, then where are we going?"

"We're going to see my best friend."

"Your best friend! I don't want to meet your best friend in jeans and a t-shirt either."

"I want you to meet my best friend."

"In jeans and a t-shirt."

"Yes! I laughed. "In jeans and a t-shirt. You're going to be fine."

The turn I needed to take was coming up. I let the top up on the car. We were about to kick up dirt. When I made the turn, the dust from the dirt started up. Five miles down the road, we saw a white stable with a green roof and doors. I turned onto a paved driveway. I parked the car. I got out and wet on the passenger side to open the door for DaNia. She got out of the car, asking questions.

"Your car is the only one here. Where is your best friend?"

"Come on, woman," I said. I walked to the front door of the stables and opened them. She walked in behind me. I heard her say,

"Wow! Horses."

My family loved our horses. They had a lot of interaction with people, especially from me and my mama. They saw me every weekend. All five of them came, sticking their heads out of their stalls to see who the new voice belonged to. I stopped at each stall to say hello.

"Hey, Dakota," I said, stopping at the first stall on my left. Across from Dakota was a stall.

"Ranger, how you doing, old man?"

Benny was next to Ranger. My mother loved him. He was our gray stallion. We had him the longest. I turned around to see DaNia petting Dakota. "I thought animals and nature weren't your things."

"I'm not crazy about them. My mother is a veterinarian. I've been around animals all my life. These horses are beautiful."

She stopped at Ranger's stall.

"My mama would love to come see them."

"We'll have to bring her out here one day."

"Of course, these are your horses," she said.

"Not all of them," I said. "Benny belongs to my mother. Dakota and Ranger belonged to my dad."

I ran my hand down Ellie's neck.

"This pretty brown and white filly was given to us last year. A family in town was moving and couldn't take her with them."

DaNia walked over to the stall across from Ellie.

"Oh my," she said

I watched the jet-black mare accept her rub down her face.

"That's Sable, my best friend."

"Really?" asked DaNia, looking at me.

"Yes. Since I can remember, my dad always had horses. I had a good relationship with them but none like I have with her."

I joined DaNia in front of the stall.

"Hey, girl," I said, rubbing Sable.

I opened the stall. "Let's get you saddled up. You wanna show DaNia how beautiful and talented you are?"

Sable never gave me problems. She gave my brothers hell. I was the only one who could saddle her up with ease. Once she was ready to go, I led her out of the back of the stables. I hopped on my girl.

"We'll be right back," I said to DaNia.

"I'll be right here," she smiled.

I started Sable out slow with a walk around the perimeter. When I felt she was ready to trot, she did. Her legs were good. We picked up the speed, and my girl showed DaNia she could be just as beautiful in the wind as she was in her stall.

I slowed her down as we got closer to Da'Nia. Sable stopped a little way in front of DaNia. I hopped down.

"Y'all were great. I took so many pictures of you."

DaNia showed me the pictures she had taken of us. My girl sable was always photogenic. DaNia had great shots of our ride.

"Those are nice," I said, taking her by her hand. "It's your turn."

"My turn," said DaNia, refusing to move.

"Yes, your turn," I laughed.

"No!" she said.

"Yes, I said, pulling her to Sable."

"Is she going to go fast?"

"No, I'll be guiding her."

"I've never rode a horse."

"I know this," I laughed. "I got you."

DaNia eyed me while we walked over to Sable. I walked her through how to get on the horse. It took her two tries, but she made it. When I started to guide Sable, she closed her eyes. I was laughing. She was cracking me up.

"Open your eyes!"

She would not open her eyes. I let her keep her eyes closed for the first ride around the white fence. On our second time around, I stopped sable.

"DaNia open your eyes."

"Am I about to get down?" she asked me.

"Yes..."

DaNia opened her eyes.

"Right after the sun sets," I said.

DaNia looked out into the fading blue sky and at the golden orange sun.

"This is beautiful."

"I know," I said. "It's been my place to clear my mind in the evening."

THE RECIPE OF A GODLY WOMAN IX: HOPE

I helped her down from Sable. Wrapping my arms around her waist, she leaned back into my body.

"I brought a beautiful woman to meet a beautiful creature and to watch a beautiful sunset," I said as we watched the rest of the sun go down.

DaNia

With his hands covering my eyes, I couldn't see where he was leading me. I was excited and ready to see what he had planned for us. I knew we were outside. Jett loved to be outside. I wasn't complaining. Him taking me out of my comfort zone ended up being the best dates.

He stopped walking, and so did I. He removed his hands from my eyes. I opened them to see we were standing in the grass near a river. There was a boat in the grass. I walked over to the boat. Inside the boat was a picnic basket and a classic red and white blanket. I turned around to see him smiling.

"Are you good with a picnic on the river?"

I thought the idea was very romantic.

"I'm good with a picnic on the river," I smiled.

We were out in the middle of the water in the boat. I could see the green grass and different colors of flowers. We had a slow float to the boat. Jett spread the blanket out in the boat. He pulled a small bag of green grapes from the basket. Sticking his hand in the bag, he pulled one out and fed it to me. It was one of the best grapes I had ever had.

"You gone feed me the whole time?" I asked him.

"I'll feed you whatever, whenever, however, you want me to."

THE RECIPE OF A GODLY WOMAN IX: HOPE

"I'm already knowing," I laughed.
"Then why ask?" he asked, moving closer to me.
"I wanted to hear yo answer," I said.
"What else you wanna hear?"
"What you wanna tell me?"

Jett was so close to me that our lips were second from touching.

"I don't wanna tell you anything. I wanna give you something."

"What you wanna give me?"

"This," he said, pressing his lips against mine. His lips were so soft that I couldn't let go. The more he kissed me, the more I kissed him back.

He then slowly pulled his lips from mine. With our foreheads resting against one another's, I opened my eyes. He lifted his head. I felt his lips grace my forehead.

LATOYA GETER

Professor Jett Davenport

I finished my last class for the day. As I was walking back to my office, I thought about DaNia. I shot her a text.

"Hey, beautiful. I know you're probably tired of my outside adventures. How about we do something more simple this weekend?"

She never took long to respond to my messages.

"Hey, handsome! I'm never tired of any adventure as long as it's with you. We can do whatever. You know I like to be dressed accordingly."

I laughed! DaNia didn't play about her clothes! I loved that she cared about her appearance. I texted her back.

"Go ahead and dress up. Nothing formal, but you can get all sexy so I can show you off when we walk in."

DaNia replied back. "Lol! Say less!"

****

The doorbell to my house rang. I walked out of my kitchen and went to the door. I opened it to see DaNia.

"Hey babe," I said, hugging her.

"Hey," she said, accepting my embrace.

THE RECIPE OF A GODLY WOMAN IX: HOPE

I took her bag from her. I closed the door behind her.

"Welcome to my place."

I slid my hand into hers. I started to show her around my two-story home. We started in the kitchen with my black and silver appliances. I leaned against my bar.

"I'm looking forward to seeing what you can do in here," I smiled.

"If you want me to cook for you, just say that," she laughed.

"What that fried chicken like?"

"Buttermilk crispy fried with collard greens and cornbread."

I bit my bottom lip and pulled her to me by her waist.

"Now, don't get in trouble, woman."

She fell back laughing.

"What will happen if I add macaroni and cheese with some yams?"

I gave her a peck on her lips.

"You cook like that if you want to. I'mma be wrapped around yo finger."

DaNia gave me a small kiss back.

"I already got you wrapped around my finger."

"Been wrapped for years!" I laughed.

DaNia started laughing. "You're a mess!"

I showed her my living room. The light gray couch with the matching dark gray pillows was simple. I knew she would walk over to my fireplace.

"Beautiful."

"I can't wait until winter," I said.

"Why? It works good, huh?"

"It does work good, but I can't wait for this winter so that I can hold you under it."

DaNia slowly turned around to me.

She smiled and said, "I can't wait either."

The three bedrooms in my house were upstairs. I took her hand and led her upstairs. I opened my bedroom door.

"You'll be sleeping in here," I said.

She looked around my bedroom.

"Looks comfy," she said, looking at my dark green and black comforter and pillows. She walked over to my black dresser, setting her purse there.

"I brought the best outfit. How long do we have before we go out?"

"You have plenty of time. It's not a set time that we have to be there. Doors open at eight and close at four. I thought it would be better for us to go tonight since it's Friday. I don't want you waking up early Sunday morning tryna rush home for church."

DaNia smiled at me.

"Thank you for taking that into consideration."

"Always."

I gave her a kiss on her cheek.

"I'll let you get settled in," I said, placing her bag on the bed. "There is plenty to eat and drink downstairs. Do whatever you need to do. I'll be in my office."

I headed down the hall to my office. I had assignments to grade. I caught up on as much grading as I could. I saw the time was eight-thirty. I got up from my desk. I headed to my bedroom to let DaNia

THE RECIPE OF A GODLY WOMAN IX: HOPE

know we would be leaving around nine-thirty. I saw my bedroom door was closed. I knocked on the door.

"You can come in," I heard her say.

I pushed the door open to see DaNia sitting on my bed. She was leaning over in a black fitted leather strapless dress, trying to strap her shoes. My entire room smelled like all kinds of fruits.

"Let me get that for you," I said.

I sat on my bed next to her. I lifted her leg. It was so smooth! I strapped her shoe and placed her leg back down.

"DaNia. Baby..."

I couldn't take my eyes off her body. She was a little thick, but the leather dress hugged her in all the right places.

"You looking real good."

"Thank you," she smiled.

Her hair was different. I liked the look. Some of her hair was down in the back, while the other was up in a curly bun.

I had to stand her up. With her hand in mine, I gave her a spin. I wanted to tap that thang behind her. It was sitting fat and right. I held it together!

"No, thank you," I said. "For this beautiful sight."

"Am I beautiful?" she teased, leaning into my chest.

"Always," I said, kissing her.

She welcomed my kiss by adding to the moment.

"Are you going to get ready?" she asked me, pulling her lips from mine.

"I am," I said.

****

Addonsdale had a couple of places for nightlife. One of those was Trey's—a locally owned bar and grill. I liked to go there on Friday nights to have a drink and chill. I would invite my brothers or meet my friends.

The parking lot was not as full as I expected it to be. I told my friends to meet us there around nine-forty-five. The dashboard of my truck read nine-fifty-five.

"A club," said DaNia, looking through my windshield at the small building.

"A bar and grill," I said.

"Why you tell me to wear something sexy?"

"It's that kinda vibe in here," I said, running my hands down my black shirt and dark denim jeans.

DaNia laughed. "So you fine?"

"Look damn good," I laughed.

I opened my door and got out.

"That's why I told you to wear something sexy. You gotta match all this."

"Whatever," she laughed.

I went over to the passenger side and opened the door for her. I helped her down, closed the door, took her hand, and we headed inside.

My two good friends were sitting at a table with their dates. I introduced DaNia to Fabien and Maddox. Fabien introduced her to his wife, Shandra. Maddox wasn't married to Rory, but she had been around for a minute.

My guys and I headed to the bar to get drinks for us and the ladies. We were standing at the bar waiting

THE RECIPE OF A GODLY WOMAN IX: HOPE

for the drinks. I could see the table from where we were. DaNia seemed to be okay talking to the ladies.

I heard Maddox say, "I'll be keeping my eyes on that young, beautiful piece of caramel, too!"

I laughed, turning around from looking at the table.

"It ain't even like that. I trust her. I was tryna make sure she was comfortable with the ladies. As you said, she is young, and she was worried about our age difference at first. On my end, she's so mature that her age doesn't even show."

"I was shocked when you said you were bringing her. It's been how long since you broke up with ole girl?"

I laughed. "Too long that you have forgotten her name."

Fabien then asked me, "How long have you been dating?"

"Going on four months," I said.

"You thinking about taking her home to Mama?" asked Maddox.

"She met Sable," I said.

"Five miles from the house!" said Fabien. "Oh yeah, you're taking her home."

"Ain't she gone be the first woman to go?" asked Maddox.

"The first and the only," I said to them.

"My guy!" said Fabien. "You got marriage on ya mind!"

"I do," I said.

The bartender sat drinks in front of us. We picked up the drinks and took them back to the table. DaNia didn't drink hard liquor. That didn't bother me. Her glass of wine did fit her personality.

I found myself in the middle of the dance floor with DaNia. Our bodies were moving in the same rhythm to "Beauty" by Dru Hill. With her arms around my neck and my hands around her waist, we stared into one another's eyes.

"I'mma give you some time to prepare," I said. Next month, I would like for you to meet Margaret Davenport."

"Meet your mom?"

"Yes."

"Okay," she smiled. "Thank you for telling me."

"You're welcome," I laughed. "I know how you can be."

She laughed and gave me a kiss. "Shut up."

I reached into my pocket. "I have something to give you."

In my hand was a key to my house.

"For when we make plans at my house. You don't have to wait for me to leave campus. You don't have to leave out early in the morning or drive late at night. You can just come when it's convenient for you."

DaNia smiled. "Okay, pressure! You applying it, ain't you?"

I had to laugh. I was applying pressure, and I wasn't letting up or going backward.

"If I'm moving too fast, let me know."

"You're fine," she said. "You just surprised me with so much in like two minutes."

I thought back to our conversation in Atlanta in the hotel room.

THE RECIPE OF A GODLY WOMAN IX: HOPE

"Remember when I told you I wasn't tryna play with your feelings or take advantage of you?"

"I remember," she said.

"I also told you I planned to show you."

"You did."

"Well, I'm showing you."

DaNia smiled, giving me another kiss.

DaNia

The street looked familiar. When I saw the stables, I knew I had been down it before. We drove a little more in his truck, and I saw a two-story, traditional, dark red brick house. The rectangle windows and dark black shutters were pretty. The tan driveway led to a two-car garage—Jett parked in the driveway. As I opened the passenger side door of the truck to get out, the front door of the house opened. A woman with a light brown complexion and dark brown hair with a tent of gray came out of the house. She wore a pair of leggings, a pink T-shirt, and tennis shoes. Jett told me to wear comfortable clothes, but she was too comfortable.

She walked over to us as the garage was coming up.

"Hey. Son," she said, hugging Jett.

"Hey Mama," he said, kissing her on her cheek.

She then made eye contact with me. She smiled so big.

"You must be DaNia."

"Yes, ma'am," I said.

She gave me a hug. "I've heard so much about you. Nice to finally meet you."

"Nice to meet you as well, Ms. Maragret."

"Nope," she smiled. "Mama Margaret."

THE RECIPE OF A GODLY WOMAN IX: HOPE

"Noted," I smiled.

"You're so beautiful," she smiled, placing her hand on my face.

"She is," said Jett.

Margaret turned around to Jett. "I see you're wrapped around her finger already."

She turned back to me with a wink. I laughed so hard. She then started to order Jett around.

"Pull the Lyriq out and put your truck in," she said, referring to her black Cadillac Lyriq.

"Yes, ma'am," he said.

She and I moved to the side while Jett moved the vehicles.

"I'm so happy I got the chance to meet you. Jett talks about you all the time. It does my heart good to listen to my son talk about a woman who brings him so much joy and happiness. I'm excited that he has found someone. My other sons have families. I was waiting for him to bring a lady to meet me."

"He does the same for me," I smiled. "I'm honored to meet you. I know he loves you dearly."

"Now, me and you get to spend the day together," she smiled.

"I'm looking forward to it," I said.

Jett pulled up to us in the Lyriq.

"You can have the front seat," she said to me. "Y'all can chauffeur me around today."

"Yes, ma'am," I laughed.

Jett got out of the driver's side.

"What you say, Mama?"

"You're driving me around today."

"Don't I always."

"Well, today you and Nia are!"

She looked at me and asked, "I can call you that?"

"Yes, ma'am," I smiled.

Jett opened the back door for his mother. He helped her in. I went ahead and got in on the passenger side.

When we passed the Addonsdale sign, I realized we were leaving the city. I turned to Jett. He didn't even let me get my words out.

"Don't get to asking me questions. Just ride."

I heard his mother snickering. I laughed before asking her,

"Mama Margaret! You know where we're going?"

"Honey, he tells me the same thing," she laughed.

Jett laughed. "Tell her to get used to it, Mama. She ain't learned yet."

The next welcome sent my nerves straight through the roof of the Cadillac! Welcome to Crestview!

"Crestview!" I said. "What are we doing in Crestview?"

"Passing through," laughed Jett.

He turned on a very familiar street.

"You're lying!" I said. "Turn around!"

He laughed and kept driving. I saw our family shelter in the distance. He pulled into the parking lot. I knew every car that was parked!

"Why is my entire family here?"

I also saw a truck that read J. Davenport Farming and Produce.

"What is going on?" I asked.

"We're at Restoration Ministries," said Jett.

"I know where we are! It's my family's non-profit shelter for the homeless!"

I heard the window being let down on my side. Looking out of it, I saw my daddy coming our way.

"Oh no," I said, pressing the button to try to let the window up. It wasn't working.

"It's locked," laughed Jett.

"This is not funny!" I laughed. "Unlock it!"

Jett wouldn't unlock the windows. I hit him so fast!

"Why are you playing?"

I hit him again.

"Hit that man one more time," said Daddy. His voice scared me! I jumped so hard. I turned around to see my daddy standing at the window.

"Hey, Daddy."

"Hey, baby girl," he smiled.

Jett unlocked the doors. Daddy opened the door for me and Ms. Margaret. He helped her down and gave me a hug. Jett had made it around the car.

"Nice to see you again, Jett," said Daddy.

I could have passed out. They knew each other. Before I could even ask questions, I heard Mama Margaret say,

"Hey, Audrey!"

I looked up to see my mama coming out of the shelter. How did Margaret know my mama?

"Woah!" I said. "What is going on?"

Daddy started up! "You didn't tell me about Jett! I had to hear about him from ya mama. I thought you loved me, baby girl," he laughed. "Daddy would do anything for his baby, and you couldn't tell me."

Jett then said, "Let me explain, baby."

"Nah!" laughed Daddy. "You ain't gotta explain nothing to her. I know she is spoiled. I spoiled her."

"That means you know about her temper tantrums," laughed Jett.

"I do know about them! You know what, you may want to explain," laughed Daddy.

"Oh, so y'all just buddy ole pals!" I laughed.

Mama gave me a hug. "It's okay, baby girl. I'mma get your daddy later."

I stuck my tongue out at my daddy.

"Get that one, too," I said, pointing at Jett.

"Naw, I like him," said Mama.

"Yeah, but I'm ya favorite," said Keys, joining us. He shook Jett's hand, introducing himself.

"He ain't the favorite," said Shaheem. "I am." He also shook Jett's hand and introduced himself.

"How are the horses?" asked Mama.

"They're doing good," said Mama Margaret.

"Mama!" I said.

Both of them turned around. I laughed, shaking my head.

"You been to the stables?"

"I have," said Mama.

"When?"

"After we went to meet Margaret."

Jett took my hand. "I set all of this up. I couldn't keep seeing you without meeting your parents. It didn't feel right. I called around, found some numbers, and came here to meet your parents."

Arbrielle and Ariel walked up. Arbrielle gave me a hug.

"You know we couldn't mind our business."

"Cause you are our business," said Ariel.

Malachi and DJ came up. DJ shook hands with Jett. "Good to see you, bro."

"We helped him get in touch with Daddy and Mama," smiled Ariel.

Jett then said, "I know how you like helping people. My family brought in produce from our farm to feed the residents of your family's shelter. We are going to cook and serve the people together."

My heart warmed. My eyes filled with tears. Jett's actions were so thoughtful and had so much meaning behind them.

"You did all of this for me while still helping others."

"Yeah," he smiled.

"Don't kiss him or cry in front of us," said Arbrielle. "Save it for when y'all are by yourself."

Everyone laughed at her. We then headed inside the shelter. My aunties were already in the kitchen prepping. I introduced them to Jett. He didn't have to tell me who the four men were. They looked just like him. He introduced me to them. All their names started with J. John Jr., Jerald, Johnathan, and Jackson.

Me and Jett always had a great time together. Everything he did for me was special, but pulling off a community service event with our families coming together to give back was by far the best thing he had ever done.

LATOYA GETER

Professor Jett Davenport

A black and gold bag sat on my kitchen table. Tied to the bags were burgundy and orange balloons. I was sitting at the table behind the bags and balloons. I heard my front door open. DaNia walked into my kitchen.

"What is this?" she asked me.

"For you," I said.

"Burgundy and orange balloons in a black and gold bag."

"Yep," I said.

"School colors. Ross and Stone."

"Yep," I said.

"Black and Gold. Graduation. I'm not graduating until May."

"Are you?"

"Am I? Huh?"

"Just open it," I said.

DaNia walked over to the side of the table. She reached into the bag, pulling out a piece of paper. Her eyes widened as she read the paper. She covered her mouth, looking at me.

"Congratulations, babe," I said.

She took her hand down from her mouth.

"Is this real?"

"Yes, babe, it's real."

THE RECIPE OF A GODLY WOMAN IX: HOPE

"I'm graduating early?"

"Yes. You're graduating a semester early—December instead of May. An email was sent out to the board and the department. Your name was on there. You should be getting your email soon."

I saw her eyes filling with tears. I got up from the table, wrapping my arms around her.

"These better be happy tears."

"They are," she said. "We still have to do our final productions."

"Check with your professors. All I know is you're graduating in December, and it's not a mistake. You know your man checked."

DaNia laughed. "Thank you, baby."

"I got you, girl," I said, leaning down to kiss her. She never hesitated to kiss me back. I unlocked my lips with her. I took her by her hand, leading her into my living room. We sat on my couch. She laid back in my arms.

"How are you feeling about graduating early?"

"I feel good. I wasn't expecting to graduate early, but it feels good. I gotta start looking for apartments."

"Why? Your parents aren't going to make you leave because you're graduating."

DaNia sat up and looked at me. "You said we would be official after I graduated. You can't be coming over to my parents' house to see me. I'm gonna eventually be working. How am I gonna keep coming over here?"

"Baby, if you're tired of driving, let me know that. You could have told me that, and we could have worked that out."

"By doing what? Are you coming to Crestview for a few hours? Me only seeing you once a week? No! I wouldn't have wanted to do that, and I don't want to do that now."

DaNia was getting worked up. There was no need for that. I had to calm down her down.

"Hey, hey," I said, kissing her. "Chill. We just found out that you're graduating early. Focus on what you have left to finish in school."

"And what?" she asked, pulling away from my kiss. "You'll handle my living situation?"

I kissed her again. "First of all, don't ever pull away from my kisses. Yeah, I'll handle it for you."

"Boy, whatever," she said, rolling her eyes.

That was my cue to get up from my couch. I was walking out of the living room when I heard her ask me,

"Where are you going?"

I turned around with my guy standing at full attention.

"To handle my business. Before I handle you."

DaNia bit her lip.

"Bye, babe, I'm going upstairs! You're playing!" I said.

"I'm sorry," she said.

"Yeah, yeah," I said, leaving the room.

THE RECIPE OF A GODLY WOMAN IX: HOPE

DaNia

I wasn't graduating early by myself. Taylor and Symone were, too! We were standing in the graduation line outside of our athletic complex. Symone was fixing my stoles. I had an honor roll stole for being an honor student. I also had a stole for my department and two honor societies.

Taylor nudged me. Our instructors were passing by and heading into the gym. Jett smiled at me. I smiled back at him. Symone laughed, shaking her head.

As soon as I stepped foot into the auditorium, Arbrielle's voice caught my ears! She was screaming so loud for me. I smiled, looking up to my right. My family was there to support me! My Aunt Allison was waving. Aunt Kim was just as loud as Arbrielle. Aunt Lauren blew me a kiss. I blew one back to my fav. Mama was leaning into my daddy. My girl was crying. Daddy's smile told me he was so proud. Malachi and DJ were standing next to Daddy, whistling. My cousins sat behind our parents with my nieces and nephews. My sister-in-law, Gigi, was sweet enough to help me and my sisters get me ready for my big day. As soon as I sat down, I heard my name echo across the gym. I looked up with a smile to see my brother-in-laws standing, flexing their muscles. I laughed, giving them a flex back.

LATOYA GETER

The Vice President of Academics approached the podium.

"This year, we are making history. We do not have a valedictorian or a salutatorian. We have five students who have maintained a 4.0 throughout their college career."

Claps echoed throughout the gym. I looked around to see almost everyone clapping.

"We do not have time for each of them to give a speech. We do want to recognize them. Students, when I call your name, please stand. Each of you will receive an honor medallion as the valedictorians and salutatorians have received at our graduations."

He announced the first and second students. He then announced the third student.

"DaNia Michelle Reynolds. Drama and theatre."

I stood up, and my family went for what they knew. They were the loudest group in the arena. I enjoyed every moment of the love shown to me. Just when I thought they couldn't get any louder, they were extremely loud when I walked across the stage to receive my degree. The one thing I loved about my family was their acceptance of those we brought into the family. They screamed just as loud for Symone and Taylor as they did for me.

The last student walked across the stage, and all of us went crazy. Students were dancing. Others were raising their degrees in the air. When we heard move your tassels from the right to the left, it got real for everyone.

We finally settled down and walked out. Taylor and I waited for Symone to come out. When she came out, we all grabbed each other, hugging one another.

Our professors started to come out of the arena. Jett came out of nowhere, wrapping his arm around me and kissing me in front of my entire class.

My family had a graduation dinner for me afterward. There were so many gifts for me. I couldn't even open them all. I had to save the rest. *While I was going through my gifts, I realized there wasn't one from Jett.* He came over to me and whispered into my ear. *His gift wasn't there. He wanted to take me to it once I finished spending time with my family.* I wanted to know what it was. I was excited to find out what he got me.

We ate and danced all night long at the party. I was surprised my mama stayed up with us until midnight. Daddy went to bed early. My family left early, too.

I actually thought it was too late for Jett to give me my gift. He said it wasn't. We walked out of my parents' house and got into the Audi. He drove to a gated apartment complex.

"You did not!" I said, realizing what my graduation gift was.

"Oh, I did," he smiled.

He parked his car and pulled out a key from his pants pocket.

"Let's go check out your apartment."

"Let's go," I smiled.

We got out of the car. Jett took my hand. He walked up on a pair of steps, and I followed. We stopped in front of a door.

"Use your key," he said.

I used the key to unlock the door. I slowly pushed the door open. I saw there was furniture already in the apartment. In the living room was a light brown sectional with power pink, dark brown, and cream fluffy pillows. There was a light pink fluffy rug in the middle of the floor.

"This big ole TV," I laughed, staring at the sixty-five-inch.

"Yeah, that's for ya, man, when I come over."

I looked at Jett and shook my head.

"What?" he laughed. "I got the apartment and everything in it. I can at least be able to watch my games after church."

I heard everything he said. Church lingered with me. Jett hadn't been to our main church or the sister church. I hadn't heard him mention a church home.

"Church," I said, walking into the kitchen. The nude polka dot theme had mama's touch to it. From the towels to the canisters. "This is my first time hearing you talk about church."

"I want to start going," he said. "Mama goes. We went as kids. I stopped going when I got older."

"Your mom's personality told me she made sure you knew of Christ."

"I'm saved," said Jett. "I need a lot of work, too."

"Don't we all," I said.

I left out of the kitchen. There were two rooms and a bathroom off from the living room. I flicked the light switch in the bathroom. I smiled cause Ariel tried to add pink marbles and nude seashells to the sea theme. She even painted ocean scenes for the wall. I loved that the coral in the paintings was pink.

THE RECIPE OF A GODLY WOMAN IX: HOPE

"I need to work on getting my life back on track. I believe my relationship with God is where I need to start. My life hasn't been the same since my father passed away," explained Jett.

Walking out of the bathroom and into a room, I flipped the light to see my guest room. I laughed at the iPad charging in the red case on the black nightstand. It belonged to my twin brother. He had something to do with the sky-blue-themed room.

"You tried to come home trying to fix everything for your mom," I said, walking out of that room.

"I did," he said, following me. "Maybe I was supposed to let God handle it. I let my career go. I stopped working toward my goals."

"Or maybe it was all in God's plan for you to sacrifice some things to do what he had for you to do. You're successful now. You've been rewarded for your sacrifice."

I knew the last bedroom was mine. I flipped the light. I loved the grand silver headboard and California king-size bed combo. I ran my hands down the pink, silky satin comforter. I looked at myself in the mirror that came with the marble dresser. I loved the small round nude rugs that were on each side of the bed. The picture on the wall stood out to me. It was of me and Jett. We were standing at the department table at the clothing drive with the campus ministry.

"You were a part of my reward," he said.

I turned around to him.

"Had I still been on the road acting, would I have received you?"

"Possibly. We could have met."

I turned back to the picture.

"You had it printed," I smiled.

"I did."

"I know my family helped you put this together."

"They did," he said.

"Who had this idea?"

"The picture was all me. Your Aunt Lauren suggested a picture of us that will remind you of our happy times when things get rough in the future."

I immediately turned around to him.

"My Aunt Lauren…"

"Yeah, so I chose a picture to help you think about where we started to lead you to all of our happy times."

I wanted to cry. I knew why my aunt suggested the picture. She told me she wanted me to live life and be happy. Knowing that she was helping the new relationship that had barely begun after I had dated her son for so long proved her words were true.

Me and Jett walked back into the living room. He didn't know it, but I was holding in all kinds of emotions. I graduated college early. I still had to return to Ross and Stone to audition for casting directors. I had a new apartment. Which meant he listened to me and handled it for me. The gesture by Aunt Lauren didn't help.

"Thank you," I said, trying not to let my tears fall.

"You're welcome, baby," he said.

Jett wrapped his arms around me. He kissed me on the cheek.

THE RECIPE OF A GODLY WOMAN IX: HOPE

"Your mama and sisters brought all your clothes. They are in your closet and dresser. If you want to stay here tonight, we'll get your car, or you can stay at your parents'. I got me and mama a hotel room. Whatever you want to do is fine."

LATOYA GETER

Professor Jett Davenport

"I wanna stay here," said DaNia.

"Alright," I said. "We can go get your car in the morning."

I leaned down, giving her a kiss goodnight. I walked to the door. I placed my hand on the knob. My shirt was being tugged.

"I want you to stay with me," said DaNia.

I slowly turned around. She moved closer to me. Our eyes were locked. She lifted her head. Her lips were close to mine. I took the kiss she was trying to give to me. Our tongues took over. My hands found her neck. Easing them down her back, my tongue graced her neck. Her grip around the back of my head was the assurance that she was already feeling good. When I started to lift her shirt, she didn't stop me. I didn't stop myself. While I caressed her waist, my lips kissed her stomach. She began to lift her shirt. She pulled it over her head, throwing it to the floor. Kissing up her stomach, I lifted her left leg. I only needed my left hand to unhook her bra. Kissing her right shoulder was a must before I pulled her bra strap down with my teeth. My tongue trailed over her nipples before I kissed her left shoulder and pulled that bra strap down with my teeth. With her bra hanging on her right wrist, I lifted her right leg. The lift into the

THE RECIPE OF A GODLY WOMAN IX: HOPE

air sent the bra strap to the floor. Her legs grew tighter around me as I kissed her body. I walked back to her bedroom with my face buried in her body.

Lying her down on her bed, I kissed her lips, her neck, her breast, and her stomach. I eased down to her waist, kissing her here. Removing her jeans, I kissed her thighs. Unbuckling my pants and allowing them to fall to her bedroom floor, I climbed back into bed with her. I lifted my shirt over my head.

I knew I was going to be in control all night. I didn't have a problem with that. I eased down into the bed, pulling her body on top of mine. Taking her right breast into my mouth while squeezing her body, I heard a moan escape her mouth. The more I pleased her, the more she moaned, but she never pulled away. I rolled her over, kissing my way down. Her body relaxing was the signal I needed to take off her panties.

This time, I eased her legs up. One day in the future, I knew she was going to either beg for me to devour her or make me. I pulled my boxers down for dessert. I was one hungry man who had been waiting on the main course for years.

I started by trailing the outside of her steaming sensation. The heat warmed my lips. I gave her a lick. DaNia's body eased up the bed a little. I couldn't have her running from my loving. Teasing her would do just that. I took her legs into the crevice of my arms and elbows, locked her down, and filled her up with my tongue. The more she moaned, the more I wanted dessert. Lifting my head from finishing dinner, I slopped up what was left of her. I needed a napkin. She was dripping down my face.

I crawled up the bed, resting between her legs. She stared into my eyes.

"Are we really here?"

She was the queen bee. I was the honey stick inches from entering her honey pot.

"We are," I said. "This moment is enough for me if you feel all the way will be too much for you."

"I know it won't be too much for me because I love you, Jett."

She was the first woman ever to tell me she loved me first. Her words sent me into overdrive, but there was no way I would drive her. My heart wouldn't let me. So, I let it take over instead.

The entrance to her whole world started to open. Her grip squeezed so tight. I didn't handle my business beforehand—shame on me. I fought the build-up. I couldn't release early. I had to make love to her.

I eased more and more. Breaking through her walls wasn't easy for me. I knew she had to be in pain. I eased down and pulled her bare body to my bareness.

"I love you too, DaNia," I said, whispering in her ear while I pushed all the way through.

THE RECIPE OF A GODLY WOMAN IX: HOPE

DaNia

Two Months Later

Carrying a bag of groceries, I got out of my car. I was walking toward my apartment. I saw a familiar face. The person looked my way. They recognized me as well.

"DaNia," said Haze.

"Haze," I said, stopping on the sidewalk of the apartment complex.

"How have you been?" he asked me.

"I'm good," I said, eyeing him.

"Why the look?" he asked me.

"Why are you in Crestview?"

"I've been here. Since August. The hospital has a program for students going into med school next year."

Haze was right. I hadn't seen him on campus. I was so into my relationship with Jett that I hadn't thought about him.

"You're here during the week. School is still in. Did you graduate early?"

"I did," I said.

"I'm not surprised. Congratulations."

"Thank you," I said. "Congratulations to you too."

"Thanks," he said. "Do you live here?"

"I do," I said. "I moved in about two months ago."

He reached for my groceries.

"Nuh-uh," I said. "You're not slick."

Haze held his hands in the air.

"I was going to take them to your apartment for you."

"No," I said. "No, thank you. I'm in a relationship."

"Your ex is better?"

"No," I said.

"Oh, someone new?"

"Yes," I said.

"Okay, that's good too. I'm in a relationship. I met her at the hospital. Actually, all of the students in the program stay in these apartments. I was coming from her apartment and decided to walk this way today. I've never been around to this side."

I was so relieved he had a girlfriend. *If he was single, I wasn't going to entertain him this time.* I felt very different about Jett. *Something was coming our way. I was not about to let another man interfere with it.*

I handed Haze the bag of groceries.

"Only because you're in a relationship."

Haze laughed. "You, of all women, should know once my mind is made up about a woman, it's not changing."

"You're right," I laughed.

"Lead the way, mane," he said, shaking his head.

****

THE RECIPE OF A GODLY WOMAN IX: HOPE

My phone was ringing. I rolled over in my bed, picking it up from the night stand.

"Hello," I said, answering the call.

"Of course, your beautiful self would be born on Valentine's Day," said Jett. "Happy Birthday, baby."

"Thank you, babe," I said, opening my eyes.

"How you feeling this morning?" he asked me.

Jett knew I hadn't been feeling well the last couple of mornings. I thought about my response. I wanted to tell him I wasn't feeling well, but instead I said,

"I'm feeling better."

"That's good," he said. "Can't have you sick on your birthday."

"If I start to feel bad," I lied. "I'll let you know."

"I'm coming later this evening when everyone meets at your parents' house."

"Okay, babe," I said. "I'm about to get up and take a shower."

I was lying. I was feeling sick. I sat up in bed, pulling the covers back. I got out of bed and walked to my bathroom.

"Okay. I love you. See you later."

"Love you too," I said, pushing my bathroom door open. I made sure my phone was hung up before I dropped my head in the toilet.

I had to get myself together. I was supposed to meet my family later that day for my birthday party. I was in and out. I was sleeping and replying to text messages. I set my alarm for six o' clock. My twenty-third birthday party was starting at seven-thirty.

When my alarm went off, I tried to get out of bed again. I made it. I took my pink sequin dress from my closet and laid it on my bed. I wanted to take a bath, but I needed the shower to wake me up. After my shower, I felt a little better. I put on my dress. I stared at myself in the mirror. I tried to give myself a pep talk.

"Just make it until he gets here. Then you can tell him."

I walked into my living room with my purse on my arm. Grabbing my keys from the key rack, I opened my apartment door, running into a chest.

"Hey baby," he said. "Happy Birthday. Happy Valentine's Day."

I stepped back, staring at Lil Greg.

I gulped so hard. "Hey," I said.

"You looking good," he said.

"Thank you," I said.

I was trying to come to terms with the fact that I was actually looking at him. How did he know where I lived? I remembered the Life 360 app. Even though it showed my location, how did he know what apartment to come to?

Lil Greg walked into my apartment.

"Where you finna go?" he asked me.

"You know we have our birthday parties at my parents' house."

"Can I go with you?"

"What kind of question is that?" I asked him. "You know you can."

"No. I don't know that," said Lil Greg.

He closed my apartment door.

"You may be going with ya lil boyfriend."

Lil Greg moved closer to me. I didn't move. He towered down over me. I looked up at him. Before I responded, I wondered how he found out about me and Jett.

"My boyfriend…"

"Yeah. The lil nigga that be bringing yo groceries up here. I know that's who you been with since I been at that facility."

He was talking about Haze. How did he know about the one time when Haze brought my groceries to my apartment?

"He's only a friend," I said. "A friend from school."

"Bull shit!" snapped Lil Greg. "You think I don't know!" he said, beginning to raise his voice. "I know!" he growled.

He didn't know anything. He thought he knew. I hated to do it, but I had to beat him at his own game. The nice and calm DaNia wasn't working. I had to break him down to calm him down.

"What do you know?" I spat back. "What bullshit do you know?"

"I know he be over here!"

"He does not!"

"Yeah, he does! My boys who got out before I did saw him over here. You ain't hard to find!"

"You had people watching me?"

"You're my woman! Hell yeah, I did!"

Lil Greg started to pace in my living room.

"You're my woman! Mine! My woman left me in a facility!"

"Left you!" I yelled. "Did I leave you? No! You left me! You left me a long time ago! I was there for you! You were hurting yourself! You were hurting me!

You were hurting us! I did not leave you! I didn't come to see you because I had to focus on me! I had school!"

Lil Greg and I were going back and forth in a yelling match. I wasn't even trying to beat him at his own game anymore. My emotions were taking over.

He stopped pacing and snapped his head my way. "I supported you through school."

"You took up my time! My grades were falling. I couldn't be there for you and try to stay in school."

We heard a knock on my door. My phone started to ring. Lil Greg went into my purse and pulled out my phone.

"My love is calling," he said.

That was Jett's contact in my phone.

"Is that nigga at the door?" asked Lil Greg.

"I don't know," I snapped.

Lil Greg ran his hand down his face.

"You're smart DaNia. If your phone is ringing and he's calling, he must be at the door."

"I don't know who is at my door."

"Go open the door," he said.

I turned to walk to my door. I saw Lil Greg pull out a gun from his back pocket.

"What are you finna do with that?" I asked.

"Don't worry about it. Go open the door for ya, boyfriend."

I had no idea who was at my door. Jett called, but he had a key. He always had something up his sleeve. I was hoping he wasn't at my door. I didn't know if Lil Greg was capable of using the gun or not.

THE RECIPE OF A GODLY WOMAN IX: HOPE

I went to the door and unlocked it. I opened it just enough to see out. Haze was standing on the other side. I didn't want to see his face any more than I wanted to see Jett. Lil Greg thought he was my boyfriend.

"Hey," I said to Haze.

"What's up, DaNia," he said. "I was stopping by to wish you a happy birthday, and I heard yelling. You good?"

I felt the gun being pushed into my back. I closed my eyes, thinking of something to say. I opened my eyes, knowing that if I said too much, Lil Greg could possibly pull the trigger.

"Thank you for the birthday wish." I smiled at him and said, "I'm good."

"You sure?" asked Haze.

"Yeah," I smiled.

"DaNia, don't think that—"

Lil Greg stepped from behind me so that Haze could see him.

"Bruh. She said she's fine."

Haze looked at me. "My bad DaNia. I see you have company."

"She does!" snapped Lil Greg. "Don't come back over here, alright? She's my woman! Been my woman and gone remain my woman."

Haze didn't break our eye contact. I looked straight into his. I needed him to pick up my hint. Meanwhile, Lil Greg was still on a tangent.

"Whatever she told you is over. I'm back. We're back together. Y'all lil fantasy is over. Ain't that right, baby?"

"Calm down, my guy," said Haze. "I'm not with DaNia. We are friends from school."

"Yeah whatever, nigga! Thank you for the birthday wish. Now, bye!"

Lil Greg closed the door in Haze's face. My phone started ringing again. Lil Greg looked at it.

"My love is calling back!"

He went to the door and opened it. He walked out of the apartment. I could hear him yelling.

"Aye! Don't call her no more either."

I couldn't see Haze, but I could hear him.

"Mane if she yo woman, gone back in there. I'm not calling her. How can I be calling her and you looking at me?"

Lil Greg came back into my apartment and closed the door. "I'm cutting this damn phone off!" He started to walk towards me. He held the phone up to me, showing a black screen. "Now it's off." He threw it into my purse.

I began to walk backward.

"You know what? That lil nigga got a point," he said. "He ain't got no phone. So, who is my love?"

I kept moving backward.

"Answer me!"

"Why?"

"Oh," he said, looking past me. "That's who it is."

He saw the picture of me and Jett on my bedroom wall from the living room. He then raised the gun, pointing it at me.

"Really..." I said with tears clouding my vision. "This what you gone do?"

"I'm the only man who will have you!"

THE RECIPE OF A GODLY WOMAN IX: HOPE

"You have a gun in my face! If you kill me, you won't be able to have me!"

We were back in the yelling match. This time, I needed somebody in the apartment complex to hear me. I needed help. *I had one thing and one thing only on my mind. I couldn't protect it at this point.*

Lil Greg smiled at me. "If I kill us both, we'll be together."

One tear fell from my right eye and down my face. I wasn't even scared. I was too hurt to be.

"Do what you gotta do," I said. "I've wanted peace for so long. I wanted us to have peace. I loved you. I love you, and this is what you do to me?"

My front door flew open. Haze rushed Lil Greg.

"Get out of here, DaNia," he yelled.

LATOYA GETER

Audrey

Everyone was at our house for DaNia's birthday party. We were waiting for her to arrive. Neither she nor Jett and his family were there. I wondered where they were. It was not like DaNia to be late for any event. She was an hour late.

My family was sitting in my dining room waiting for her. I called her phone. She didn't answer. Her sisters called her. They couldn't get her on the phone. Her brothers tried to call her. No answer. Her friends were there to celebrate with her. They tried to call. DaNia wasn't answering any of our calls. We then heard a phone ring. Everyone looked around to see whose phone was ringing.

"It's me," said Lauren. She looked at her phone. "The facility is calling me."

Lauren answered the call.

"Hello...yes, this is she...he did what? What? How? When?....No! He hasn't checked in with me."

Lauren started to stare into space. She took her phone down from her ear. She began to tap her phone screen.

"Baby," said Cornelieus. "What's wrong?"

"Lil Greg checked himself out of the facility today. They couldn't stop him because he had improved. He was supposed to check in with me two hours ago!

They gave him his things back. If he has his phone, I have his location on the app."

Lauren's eyes were glued to her phone.

"Oh my God," she said. "He's at DaNia's apartment."

My husband and sons didn't waste any time. Daniel grabbed his keys, and they were out the front door. Ariel and Arbrielle agreed to stay with the rest of the family. My sisters and I got into Kim's car. We followed the guys.

We didn't even park the vehicles. We stopped them right in front of the apartment complex. Daniel and Cornelius were out of the truck first. Me and Lauren hopped out of Kim's car right behind them.

We saw DaNia running down the steps.

"Daddy! Lil Greg has a —"

We heard a gunshot. DaNia stopped on the stairs. She turned around and ran back up the steps.

"No, DaNia!" yelled Daniel.

My husband was running up the steps when we made it to the steps. We ran up as DaNia was going back into the apartment. Her scream made me run faster. We ran into the apartment to see her falling to the floor.

"Haze," she cried, taking him into her arms. The young man had been shot in his stomach.

"I'm so sorry," she cried. "Haze."

He was struggling to breathe. I ran over to them. Cornelius and Daniel were standing in front of Lil Greg.

"Big C!" said Lil Greg.

"What's up, Big G," said Cornelius. "Let me get that gun off you."

"Are you proud of me?

"I've been proud of you since I came into your life."

"What about now? You proud of this?"

"Oh, this. It was a mistake. A mistake that we're going to help you work out."

"You sure?"

"Yeah, I'm sure. Just give me the gun."

Lil Greg refused to give Cornelius the gun.

DaNia looked at her brothers for help with Haze. "We gotta get him out of here," she cried. Malachi and DJ were on their way over to us. Lil Greg pointed the gun our way.

"Why are you still talking about him?"

My husband stood in front of us, shielding us from the gun.

"Son," said Lauren, slowly walking over to Lil Greg.

"Don't even worry about him. That's done. We got to get you out of here before the police come. You shot him. People heard the shot. I know somebody has called the police."

"They just gone take me back to the facility. I don't want to go back there. I want to stay here with DaNia."

"They can't take you if you aren't here by the time they get here. Give me the gun so we can fix this."

"Fix this!" he snapped. "How? Mama, you sent me away the first time! Are you trying to trick me? You've turned on me, too?"

THE RECIPE OF A GODLY WOMAN IX: HOPE

"Give me the gun, son," said Lauren.

"No! You're turning on me like DaNia!"

Lil Greg aimed the gun at Lauren. Cornelius hit him with a hard right punch. The gun slid out of his hand and across the floor. Daniel kicked the gun away. Lil Greg was sitting on the floor laughing. Malachi and DJ were lifting Haze off the floor. We could hear sirens moving closer.

Lauren stared at Lil Greg sitting on the floor with no remorse for his actions.

"My son," she said. "My only son." Cornelius eased her away. Daniel was helping

the boys with Haze. I was helping my baby girl up from the floor when she said,

"He has another gun!"

I looked his way. Lil Greg stood up, placing the gun under his chin. Lauren turned around.

"I don't want to be here if I can't have her," he said before pulling the trigger. Blood splattered across the wall of the apartment.

"Lil Greg!" screamed DaNia. "Noooo!"

She cried, crawling toward his body. Daniel ran over to her. He picked her up from the floor. She screamed and screamed with tears falling down her face. She reached for his body. She called out his name.

I watched my best friend open her eyes. She wiped her son's blood from her face. She stared at his body. She turned around without a tear and walked out of the apartment.

The firefighters and police officers rushed in. My husband and I were able to get DaNia out of the apartment. On our way out, I grabbed her purse. We put her in the car with us. She sat between me and Lauren.

"We gotta go to the hospital with Haze," she cried.

"Audrey, where to?" asked Kim.

"To the hospital with Haze."

DaNia took her phone out of her purse. I saw she had to power it on. She wasn't answering our calls because her phone was off. Her phone immediately started to ring. I could see her screen. It read, "My Love."

"Hey babe," she said, crying. I then heard her say, "Mama Margret."

She paused and was quiet. She then let out another scream.

"What? No! No! No!"

She started to cry some more. I took the phone from her.

"Margaret."

"Hey, Audrey," said Margaret. I could hear that she was crying by the sound of her voice.

"What's wrong?" I asked her.

"Jett has been in a bad accident. He was driving his car in front of us. A truck was speeding down the highway. It hit another truck. The driver lost control and hit Jett. His car flipped twice."

"What!" I said, trying my best to control my emotions. "Where are you?"

"At the hospital?"

"Here in Crestview?"

"Yes."

"We're on our way."

THE RECIPE OF A GODLY WOMAN IX: HOPE

I called my husband to deliver the news. I then called Ariel and Arbrielle to update them. Kim dropped me and DaNia off at the emergency room. My husband was waiting at the door for us. We rushed through the double doors. We saw Margaret and her sons sitting in a corner. DaNia ran over to her. Margaret stood up, taking my baby girl in her arms. DaNia cried on her shoulders. Margaret wiped her own tears while consoling my baby.

I saw Ariel and Arbrielle coming into the emergency room. DaNia's friends Symone and Taylor were with them. DaNia fell into Ariel's arms. My oldest held her little sister. Arbrielle rubbed her back. I wrapped my arms around Margaret.

"He's going to pull through this," I said.

We heard the nurse call the last name Davenport. We all looked her way. She walked over to us.

"Hello. I'm so sorry for what has happened to your loved one. We are treating him."

She was holding a small velvet black box in her hand. She stepped forward with it.

"We wanted this in the hands of the family so that we know it's safe."

"What's that?" asked DaNia.

None of us responded to her. Margaret took the box from the nurse.

"Thank you so much."

"You're welcome," said the nurse. "The doctor will be out with an update?"

DaNia asked again. "What is that?"

Ariel turned her face to her. DaNia moved her head away.

"Mama Margaret. What is that?"

Tears fell from Maragret's eyes as she looked at DaNia. Everyone knew what was in the box except for DaNia.

"Is that a ring?" asked DaNia with tears falling down her face.

None of us said a word. We were silent. DaNia turned to her sisters.

"Was Jett gonna propose to me?"

Arbrielle looked away with tears in her eyes.

"Did you tell him?" asked Ariel.

DaNia didn't answer her question. She asked her own.

"Was he planning to propose?"

Ariel's eyes filled with tears. "You didn't tell him, did you?"

DaNia began to fall to the floor.

"Oh God!" she screamed out in tears. "He was going to propose to me."

My husband picked her up before she hit the floor.

"I can't do this by myself," she cried out. "This wasn't supposed to happen like this."

DaNia laid her head on her daddy's chest, crying her heart out.

THE RECIPE OF A GODLY WOMAN IX: HOPE

DaNia

My apartment was a crime scene. I couldn't go back there with the blood all over the walls. This was the apartment the man I was in love with purchased for me, along with everything I needed. He was in the hospital in critical condition. The blood on the walls belonged to my best friend and ex-boyfriend, who I still had love for. I wasn't ready to lose him. I didn't ever think I would witness him kill himself, but I did. I never expected Haze to get caught up in my life, but he did. I hated that. He had changed and didn't deserve to be shot. He shouldn't have been lying in the hospital fighting for his life because of my mess.

All these things and more were running through my mind as I laid in my bedroom at my parents' house. The more I thought about Lil Greg, the more I cried. The more I cried, Haze crossed my mind. Jett he never left my heart, mind, and soul. I was all over the place. There was only one person who I needed to talk to. I hadn't talked to them in a long time.

The next morning, I woke up still feeling the same. I felt like I needed to talk to somebody. Ariel and Arbrielle knew my truth. I hadn't told anybody else. Well, there was one other who I knew. I needed to talk to them. When I found the strength to get out of bed, it was close to evening. I showered, got dressed, grabbed my keys, and left my parents' house.

I pulled open the stable doors. Just like they did the first time I met them, the horses came to the front of their stalls to see who was there. I walked down to Sable's stall. Jett said she gave everybody a hard time when they tried to saddle her. I was ready to see how she would respond to me. I opened the stall. She stepped back, allowing me in. I raised my hand. She let me rub her face.

"Hey, pretty girl," I said to her.

To my surprise, she allowed me to saddle her with ease. I led her out of the back of the stable. *I couldn't ride her if I wanted to. It wasn't safe.* I walked her to the spot where Jett took me to watch the sun set. I looked up, and the sun was in deed setting. The sunset allowed me to think with a clear mind. I needed to talk to God. I lowered my head, closed my eyes, and I began to pray.

"Dear God,

I have put my hope in people. Lil Greg, Haze, and even Jett. I failed to put my hope in you. I don't have much left. I know that I don't need much faith, but I want you to know that I'm sorry for not putting my hope, faith, and trust in you. Even though I only need mustard seed faith, I shouldn't give you my last. You have been too good to me. You have blessed me with so much.

I've sinned. The consequences of my sin are here. I can't change it. I can only hope that you allow it to be my light of new hope.

THE RECIPE OF A GODLY WOMAN IX: HOPE

I hope and pray that you have mercy on Lil Greg's soul. He was so damaged and lost. I don't think I made things any better. Mama told me to give the situation over to you, and I didn't listen. I knew better than to give Haze false hope. I shouldn't even have been his friend. He wouldn't be in the situation. Jett was the one I hoped for, and now he is fighting for his life. I'm handing it all over to you. Whatever your will is, let it be done. I will no longer put my hope in people or situations. My hope, faith, and trust is in you."

LATOYA GETER

Audrey

The elevator door opened. Margaret and I stepped off. We walked down the hospital hallway that led to Jett's room. He had been in the hospital for a month. Margaret never left Crestview. She stayed by her son's side. I was right there with her. We even allowed her to stay in one of our extra rooms. Her other sons continued to care for the farm and horses.

We walked into the room. Margaret saw that his eyes were open. She ran over to the bed.

"Praise God," she said. "Hey, son!"

I noticed there were no more tubes in his mouth. The nurse walked in and said, "We were just about to call you. We are surprised to see him up. We got the okay to remove the breathing tubes."

"God is a good God," said Margaret, pulling up a chair next to the bed. She rubbed her hand down her son's head. My heart filled with so much joy.

We noticed his lips were moving. He was trying to speak. We paid close attention to him. His voice was raspy, but I heard him clearly.

"DaNia."

I moved closer to the bed. "You want DaNia?"

He nodded his head yes. I took out my cell phone from my purse. I dialed her number, placing her on speaker.

THE RECIPE OF A GODLY WOMAN IX: HOPE

"Hey, Mama," she answered.

Jett heard her. Her voice made him smile. He lifted his hand as if he wanted the phone. I moved the phone closer to him.

"Mama," said DaNia. "Hello."

Jett opened his mouth to speak again.

"Hey, beautiful…"

"Hello…" she said. I could tell she was trying to figure out if it was really his voice she was hearing.

"Hey beautiful…" he said again.

"Baby! Jett!" she screamed with all the excitement her body could hold.

"Yes," I said, speaking into the phone. "He is up. No tubes. They're gone."

"I'm on my way up there," she said.

"Be careful, DaNia."

"Yes, ma'am," she said. "I'll see you in a minute."

It didn't take long for DaNia to get to the hospital. I told her to be careful. When she got there in twenty minutes, I thought she had sped until I saw her sisters with her. Arbrielle was the speeder. She definitely was the one behind the wheel.

Jett smiled at her as she walked through the door. She rushed over to the bed.

"Hey baby!" she said.

"Hey, babe," he said, clearing his throat.

"Don't try to talk as much," she said.

"I can't feel…" he said.

I lowered my head. Margaret had already been informed by the doctor of possible paralysis. DaNia turned our way.

"Do we need to call a nurse?"

"No," said Margaret. She hadn't told DaNia. I didn't think the timing was good. *DaNia didn't know that I knew her situation. But I did. I was her mother.*

Margaret looked at me for confirmation. I nodded my head to break the news.

"You're paralyzed, son," said Margaret.

Jett had no words. He blinked his eyes four consecutive times before looking away from his mother. One tear fell from his left eye. DaNia pulled up a chair to the hospital bed.

"Babe..." she said to him.

He didn't turn back her way.

"Baby..." she said again.

A tear fell from his right eye. DaNia wiped the tear, and more came. Jett looked up at the ceiling. He was so angry. The veins in his neck began to show as he tightened his fists with tears flowing down his face.

"Hey, hey," said DaNia, turning his face toward her.

"What?" he said in a raspy voice. "I'm paralyzed."

"You're here," said DaNia, with tears filling her eyes.

"Barely," he snapped. "I'm literally half of a man. I'm not gonna be able to be the man you need me to be. You want a husband and children. I can't give you that now."

DaNia set her purse on the bed. "You may not be able to give me child now, but that's okay."

"No, it's not," said Jett.

"Yes, it is," said DaNia, reaching into her purse. "You've already given me one."

THE RECIPE OF A GODLY WOMAN IX: HOPE

My daughter pulled out an ultrasound. I knew she was pregnant. I was waiting for her to let it be known. I also knew her sisters knew. They were too close for her not to tell them.

More tears fell down Jett's face. "You're pregnant."

"I am," smiled DaNia. "That's why I was sick. I was going to tell you at my birthday party."

DaNia took Jett's hand.

"You can't give up hope. Our child is going to need you," she said, wiping his tears. *"I know that you were going to propose to me. The nurse brought us the ring from your pocket. I'm going to need my husband when you get out of here. Paralysis is not going to stop me from loving you. We're going to figure this out together."*

DaNia smiled at him. She leaned forward, giving him a kiss.

Malachi

Seven months later

I stood before the congregation to give the sermon. It was a special day. I was celebrating the anniversary of becoming a minister. My family was there to support me. Not only was my immediate family there, but so were my in-laws. It was good to see everyone.

"It is only befitting that I return to a special message. You all have heard it before. I would ask you who you think preached it better, me or my father..."

I heard laughs throughout the congregation. My father, who was sitting behind me to my left in the pulpit, then said,

"Watch out now, son. You don't always want to know the truth."

I laughed and continued with my message.

"It doesn't matter who preached it because it was from God, so the message was clear. It's really the question of did you get it?"

I loosened my tie and moved the microphone to make sure I could be heard.

"If you didn't get it, my father and I have both preached about the recipe of a Godly woman. The ingredients are as follows: virtuous, forgiving, imperfect, honest, confirming, and complete. She understands that vengeance is not hers and that God's mercy endures forever. Today, I am going to add *hope* to that list. *Romans 8:18-25 tells us about present suffering and future glory. Godly women suffer now for the glory later. It is her hope that gets her the glory."*

A Godly woman loves people. She believes in people. She has hope in people. Hope that they can change. Hope that their situation will be better. She may even hope that a man is the one for her.

A woman of God is also human. Each of us can be blinded by the devil. He can make a situation appear to look as if it's going to change into something greater. He enjoys giving us false hope. A woman of God can fall victim to false hope. She can also lose her hope. Why does she lose hope? She loses hope because she has placed her hope in people or situations alone. The devil loves to attack people and is present in situations where he thinks God is not. An attack from the devil can have you feeling all hope is lost. But even in her darkest times, the Godly woman has hope. She is a child of God. *Proverbs 23:18 tells us, "There is surely a future hope for you, and your hope will not be cut off.*

But what kind of hope is this? It is hope in God. Not hope in people or situations. We all have placed our hope elsewhere instead of in God. Once we put our hope in God, He will bring us out of dark situations. He will begin to rain down blessings. Psalm 147:11 tells us, *"The Lord delights in those who fear him, who put their hope in His unfailing love."*

LATOYA GETER

Pastor Reynolds

Just like I did with this familiar sermon, my son ended with a story. There was a teenage girl. She thought she knew love. So she placed her hope in the one she loved. As she grew older as a woman of God, things started to happen with the one she loved. Things she couldn't handle. The hope that she had in their relationship started to fade. Another guy started to look appealing to her. She didn't like his ways. She then placed her hope in him. The hope was that he would change. Another guy came into the picture. This was the one she had hoped for. Everything was going great. Just when things were going great, the devil appeared. That's just like the devil. To show up to do damage. He worked through the first man she loved. His actions caused harm to the second man. While the devil was causing so much havoc in one area, he managed to do more in another. The third man was in a life-threatening car accident. Not only did the woman of God watch her first love commit suicide and shoot her friend, but she didn't know if the third man would live. She was carrying his unborn child, conceived out of wedlock. Her situation was terrible. She was losing hope, but she hadn't lost it all. She was a child of God. Once she placed her hope in God, light started to come into the situation. *Romans*

15:13 tells us, "May the God of hope fill you with all joy and peace as you trust in Him, so that you may overflow with hope by the power of the Holy Spirit."

The Godly woman had to recharge her hope. She had a talk with God. After that talk with Him, her spirit was filled with hope. She didn't lose hope when she found out the third man was paralyzed from the accident. She trusted in God. *Romans 12:12 tells us to "be joyful in hope, patient in affliction, and faithful in prayer."* That was a hard time for her. She was living in affliction and navigating sin, but she remained faithful in prayers to God.

LATOYA GETER

DaNia

I wasn't expecting the sermon from Malachi to be about my life. I couldn't say I didn't need it because I did. I was trying so hard to navigate the new journey of accepting my sin while supporting the father of my child. He was right. I never stopped praying. God allowed me to carry my son for the entire pregnancy. He also brought Jett home. He was in a wheelchair, but he was living and well.

As I sat in the church after my brother finished the sermon, I felt water running down my leg.

"Oh God," I said.

Jett, who was sitting on the end of the pew in his wheelchair, turned to me, "What's wrong?"

"My water just broke," I said.

My sister, Ariel, who was sitting next to me, stood up. My mother turned around and stood up. She and Margaret took my hands, leading me out of the sanctuary.

****

When we got to the hospital, I went right back to labor and delivery. My mother wasn't happy to hear there was a shortage of doctors who could deliver. While I was lying in the bed fighting contractions, a

THE RECIPE OF A GODLY WOMAN IX: HOPE

nurse came in. She said there were some student doctors available. My mother definitely wasn't happy to hear that. I really didn't care who delivered my baby. I was in too much pain to even think about it.

When it was time for me to push, Jett sat next to the bed, holding my hand. My Mother and Margaret were on the other side of the bed. My mother was rubbing my hand while Margaret rubbed my shoulders. The nurse walked in first,

"We have a student doctor about to come in."

"I don't care," I said to her.

The door opened. *Haze walked in green scrubs.*

"Haze…" I said.

"Hey, DaNia," he said. "I had to come deliver the baby of the friend who saved my life."

"Thank you so much," I said.

"You're welcome," he said, sitting down on a stool. "Let me get a push from you."

Squeezing my hands, I gave a big push.

LATOYA GETER

Audrey

Johven was born weighing 8 pounds. My new grandbaby was a big, chunky boy. Ariel blessed me with our adopted grandsons, but Johven was my first biological grandson. Me and Daniel spoiled him so. We picked up a tradition with our grandchildren. As long as we were living, we would be responsible for paying for their first, sixteenth, eighteenth, and twenty-first birthdays. Just as we paid for Galani's and baby Audrey's first birthday, we had to pay for Johven's first birthday. Like all parties, it was held at our house. Everyone came!

We all stood around the table in the dining room singing Happy Birthday to the birthday boy while he was sitting in the middle of the table in his eating chair. He clapped his hands with us after we finished. Granny's big boy was so smart.

DaNia placed a piece of cake in front of him. He wouldn't eat it. He was shaking his head no. I laughed so hard. Jett wheeled around the table with a bowl of ice cream.

"Watch him eat this."

DaNia laughed. "And you gone be changing that diaper!"

"Nah, Daddy, don't change diapers."

"You just contribute to the blowouts!"

THE RECIPE OF A GODLY WOMAN IX: HOPE

"That's just him growing into a man, baby," laughed Jett.

"Yeah, whatever," laughed DaNia.

Jett was right. Johven stuck his hands in the ice cream and stuffed his face. DaNia shook her head.

"Look at him. He doesn't even care about it being cold!"

"Eating like a grown man!" said Jett. "That's my son!"

"I'm going to go get the gifts," said DaNia.

"I'll help you," said Ariel.

When DaNia and Ariel came back into the dining room with the gifts, the family was standing around our dining room table. Jett sat in his wheelchair in front of the table. DaNia stopped, staring at us all. Everyone was quiet. As she always did, she had to ask a question.

"What's going on?"

Jett reached into his pocket. He placed the small black velvet box in his lap. Ariel smiled. DaNia closed her eyes, and the tears started. Ariel took the bags from her. Arbrielle walked over to Ariel, taking the bags. Jett locked the wheelchair. My husband walked over and stood beside him. Jett gave the ring to Daniel. He placed his hands on the armrests of the wheelchair and began to push up. DaNia covered her mouth in disbelief with her trembling hand. Jett was able to stand up. Daniel handed him the ring. He opened it, and there was a diamond ring. He took a step toward DaNia. More tears fell down her face. He walked over to her and took her hand.

"I gave up hope a year ago when I discovered I was paralyzed. Truthfully, I was still scared even after you told me you were pregnant with Johven. *Your hope and faith in God helped me get a second opinion.* I would hear you praying for me when you came to the house to help me. You went back to audition for roles. You had so many roles to choose from to start your career. *Instead, you chose to direct Drew's play.* You even told him to have it in nearby cities so that you could come home to help me and be able to care for our son. While you were on the road, I was at physical therapy learning how to walk again. You have supported me. You have been so strong and a great mother. You have prayed for me. You have placed your hope, faith, and trust in God. I need to do the same. I don't see myself becoming whole without you. I can't be whole with you as my girlfriend or just the mother of my child. I'm hoping that God has revealed to you that I am the man who is your husband. Will you marry me?"

DaNia removed her trembling hand from her face. "Yes, I will marry you," she said.

Jett wiped her tears. She looked down as he placed the ring on her finger. The two shared a kiss. My family began to celebrate with them by clapping and cheering. When everyone stopped, we heard small hands clapping. Jett and DaNia turned around to see Johven in his seat, still clapping. They both laughed. Jett walked over to the table. Johven reached for him. Jett picked him up. DaNia joined them, kissing their son on the cheek.

THE RECIPE OF A GODLY WOMAN IX: HOPE

The End.

About The Author

LaToya Geter has ranked in Amazon's Top 100 for African American Christian Fiction since 2019. She loves writing the genre. Over the years, she has learned that writing the genre is her calling. LaToya is the daughter of the late Romunda Owens and the granddaughter of the late Betty Williams. She is forever grateful for her mother's and grandmother's support during their time with her. They are her inspiration. She is a native of Little Rock, Arkansas. She enjoys spending time with the love of her life, Deddrick, and her two dogs, Ace and Charlie. LaToya established the Betty and Romunda Herman Foundation to help the educational needs of Pre-K students in Little Rock. LaToya believes, "If you take a leap of faith, you won't fail."

THE RECIPE OF A GODLY WOMAN IX: HOPE

Books By the Author

A Taste Of Esther's Stream

A simple love story! While fulfilling a mission for his father at a local youth center, Shawn finds himself falling for the youth center's director, Elicia. Shawn never expected to enjoy volunteering. He sure did not expect to fall in love. With the wisdom of his father, he learns exactly why he fell for her. Elicia has the characteristics of Esther. Shawn took his time to get to know her so, he did not mind waiting until the right time to have his first taste of Esther's stream.

Ava's Fight

While deployed in the Army, Luke McIntosh makes sure he communicates with his daughter Haleigh as much as he can! He develops a perception about her second grade teacher through their talks about her progress in school. When meeting Mrs. Ava Morgan in person for the first time, he realizes his perception did not do her justice! It was love at first sight for him! He was so in love that he was searching for the missing wedding ring that was not on her finger. It was not love at first sight for Ava. She was guarded, hurt, and ill. She was giving up on life. She had been fighting an uphill battle for so long that she refused to continue to fight. Once Luke discovers she is up against a plethora of issues, he talks a good game about fighting with her. Luke is faced with not only fighting with her. He is faced with fighting for her, losing himself while fighting and losing her to the fight. Will Luke help Ava fight until the end or will he cause her to give up near the finish line?

Made in the USA
Columbia, SC
23 October 2023